© Nick Turner

Helen Gordon lives in London and is a former associate editor of *Granta* magazine. *Landfall* is her first novel.

Landfall

HELEN GORDON

PENGUIN BOOKS

PENGUIN BOOKS

Published by the Penguin Group
Penguin Books Ltd, 80 Strand, London WC2R ORL, England
Penguin Group (USA) Inc., 375 Hudson Street, New York, New York 10014, USA
Penguin Group (Canada), 90 Eglinton Avenue East, Suite 700, Toronto, Ontario, Canada M4P 2Y3
(a division of Pearson Penguin Canada Inc.)
Penguin Ireland, 25 St Stephen's Green, Dublin 2, Ireland (a division of Penguin Books Ltd)
Penguin Group (Australia), 250 Camberwell Road, Camberwell, Victoria 3124, Australia
(a division of Pearson Australia Group Pty Ltd)
Penguin Books India Pvt Ltd, 11 Community Centre, Panchsheel Park, New Delhi – 110 017, India
Penguin Group (NZ), 67 Apollo Drive, Rosedale, Auckland 0632, New Zealand
(a division of Pearson New Zealand Ltd)
Penguin Books (South Africa) (Pty) Ltd, Block D, Rosebank Office Park, 181 Jan Smuts Avenue,
Parktown North, Gauteng 2193, South Africa

Penguin Books Ltd, Registered Offices: 80 Strand, London WC2R ORL, England

www.penguin.com

First published by Fig Tree 2011
Published in Penguin Books 2012
001

Typeset by Palimpsest Book Production Limited, Falkirk, Stirlingshire
Printed in Great Britain by Clays Ltd, St Ives plc

ISBN: 978-0-241-95442-3

www.greenpenguin.co.uk

Penguin Books is committed to a sustainable
future for our business, our readers and our planet.
This book is made from Forest Stewardship
Council™ certified paper.

ALWAYS LEARNING   **PEARSON**

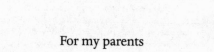

For my parents

Part One

'Most people at one time or other of their lives get a feeling that they must kill themselves; as a rule they get over it in a day or two.'

How Girls Can Help to Build Up the Empire: The Handbook for Girl Guides

(1912)

Alice thought she saw Janey sitting ahead of her on the plane from New York. For a moment the impression was so strong that Alice almost called out, even though she knew it couldn't have been her sister. The woman had the same hair as Janey; that was all. When they were very small Alice had looked at their hair – Janey's long and blonde and floating; Alice's a thick, dark block – and decided that her sister must have been adopted, and for days afterwards Janey had hidden every time the doorbell rang, convinced that her real parents were coming to take her away.

She put down her book, got up and walked along the aisle to the toilet, and then turned at the last moment to look back at the woman. It was not her sister. She was surprised, after all the years, that the feeling of disappointment was so swift, so visceral. Alice remembered how for some time after Janey had gone their mother and father had come to seem a little ghostlike, how sometimes she'd found herself flinching from their searching glances, their endless whispering and their sticky eagernesses. One Saturday she watched her father walking to the postbox and noticed the way his huge hands hung down, the empty palms turned backwards as if waiting for someone to run up and take hold of them. At the time Alice thought this was meaningful. Later, when she found a small photograph taken on a family holiday in Cornwall, from the time before her sister was gone, she realized instead that her father had always walked that way.

Returning to her row of seats, Alice climbed over the legs of the middle-aged American woman sitting by the aisle and leaned to watch the towering clouds forming beyond the small windows, each one, white tinged with lavender and pink, like a beautiful idea that hovered teasingly just out of reach. The American began talking – about the psychiatry conference she was flying to Munich to attend, about her two brothers and her nieces, about her Blue Persian that had gone into a cattery in Denver while she was away. Despite the journey, the crushed and stuffy cabin, the American's hair bore all the markings of the salon she must have visited before the flight, with the blonde tints carefully woven between the grey, the scissor marks still visible, almost. The woman glanced at Alice, at her uncombed hair, bare face and bitten nails. Only men, the American said, could be so casual when they were no longer young. Alice, who was thirty-four but often told she looked younger (excepting the lines around her eyes when she smiled), couldn't decide whether she was being commended or admonished.

'And what is it you do?' the American said.

'I'm a journalist. I write for, it's an arts and culture magazine, *Meta*. And other places, some of the broadsheets . . .'

'*Meta*? I think I've heard of that. What did you say your name was?'

'Alice Robinson.'

The American frowned. 'No . . .'

Alice made a *fuggedaboutit* gesture. For some years now her writing in *Meta* had been considered 'influential' in the art world, and her reviews in the national papers regularly sent the public out to one or another exhibition, but she never particularly expected her name to be recognized outside of those places.

She leaned back and when she looked again through the window the clouds had parted to reveal the sea; the big, heavy silvered weight of it, and here and there the white tops of the waves like the bottoms of clouds that had drifted down to float and bob on the surface. She looked out at the empty, empty water and longed to see something: a boat, a piece of bright drifting plastic. The sea had always looked the same everywhere for ever; the water she looked at now might never have been touched by humans, and all at once this seemed terrible to her.

The cabin jolted suddenly, rattling the ice cubes in the plastic cups, and the pilot's muffled voice came over the intercom. Turbulence. Alice and the American fastened their seat belts. The plane shook again and towards the rear of the cabin someone shrieked once, a guilty, choked-off sound. The American gripped the armrests until the skin around her fingernails whitened. The balding man sitting across the aisle glanced around suspiciously as though his neighbours might be somehow better informed, privy to some advance knowledge. Alice shut her eyes and thought about New York and the man with the drooping brown hair that reminded her of a singer she liked.

After the last private view she'd ended up by herself searching for somewhere new to drink and had followed two girls in matching berets to a large bar that looked like a youth club, with sweeping graffiti on the walls and rows of pool tables. She'd fallen into conversation with the man, the only other person alone and too old to be there, and they'd sipped bottles of weak beer while they played pool. Every time he smoothed down his hair – before he drank, before he played a shot – she saw the gold of the ring on his wedding finger. He had a car and they drove for hours through the half-sleeping city and he took her down through the Bronx to where they could see across the blackness of the water to Hart Island, where the unclaimed dead were buried in rows by convicts, fourteen to a trench. It was cold and they sat inside the car with the engine running. 'The Isle of the Dead,' said Alice. He took a mint out of his pocket and looked at her blankly. 'It's a painting by Arnold Böcklin. You can see it at the Met.' He shook his head. When they kissed it was like being a teenager again with nowhere to go, and his arm was an unknown weight across her shoulders. This, she thought, is how made-for-television police dramas begin. She liked his hair. Later, after he'd dropped her off near her friend

Sophie's apartment, where she was staying, she bought a hot dog from an all-night store and the steam from the food mingled with the steam from her mouth and rose like a screen in front of her face.

Sophie, who was half French and half American, was living temporarily in a quarter of a rented brownstone with her husband, Philip. She was a doctor and a volunteer with Médecins Sans Frontières. Sophie made Alice feel small and useless. 'You make me feel like a parasite,' she said to Sophie over too many glasses of wine at a local bar. 'Come the revolution and I'm first to the wall. Actually, I wouldn't even waste the bullets. Maybe I could, you know, club myself to death on the bricks or something.' She knocked her forehead against the tabletop and the pale, greenish wine trembled in their glasses.

Sophie sighed. 'I'm worried about Philip,' she said. 'He still hasn't found any work. All he does is mope around the house and watch porn on the Internet. A fact he somehow thinks he's successfully hiding from me. I used to complain about that ad agency – you know, all the brightly coloured sofas and young interns and games rooms and the creativity-inspiring bar – but now I just wish he was back there. Last week, when I told him to think about retraining, he ate a whole loaf of white bread and wouldn't speak for the rest of the evening.'

Alice nodded, rubbing her forehead. In London, *Meta* was losing advertising revenue almost daily. She seemed to know a lot of people who now wanted to get into teaching.

'How's Peter?' said Sophie, changing the subject. 'Is his flat still disgusting? I think it was living with Peter's kitchen hygiene that convinced me to give up my student lifestyle and get married. You can tell Peter that I blame him entirely for my marriage to a carbo-hydrate coma.'

'He's well. He's good. He's dating this Polish art student called Anka. She wears a broken stiletto on one foot to remind her of the suffering of the Polish dockers. She's, like, twenty-four or something.'

Sophie snorted. 'It won't last.'

'Why?'

'Because Peter's in love with you, of course. You know he's been in love with you since *for ever*.'

Alice had shrugged. People were always telling her that she and Peter were in love.

In the cabin the little Space Invader icon marking their progress from New York inched its way across a monitor suspended from the ceiling. The plane seemed to dip slightly and then settled down like an old ship falling into a comfortable trough in a stormy sea. Alice opened her eyes and tried to read. The American stretched, yawned, her breath smelling slightly doggy as she leaned over to read the book jacket. 'J. B. Priestley's *English Journey*?' she said. She shook her head and settled back to tell Alice just how ridiculous it was to talk of journeys, which imply distance and perhaps transformation, when the entire country was smaller than Florida. 'An English stroll,' she said, and snorted. 'An English hop.' The English, she said, suffered delusions of grandeur, behaving as though the northern end of their country was somewhere in the Arctic and the southern submerged in the tropics.

They were late arriving in Munich because of the bad weather, and Alice had to run to catch the connecting flight to London. ('So much cheaper than going direct,' her editor had said. 'You don't mind, do you?') Hot and red-faced she found her seat, ordered a gin and tonic when the trolley came round and then dozed a little. When she woke and glanced out of the window she saw, hazed with fog, the island itself drifting into sight. The white cliffs were smudged with drizzle, caught in the act either of pushing up from the sea, like a swimmer surfacing, or of slumping, defeated, into the iron greyness. The coast was serpentine. Fog and bad weather made the edges of the island treacherous, difficult to approach by

7

water. Lighthouses, buoys, beacons, foghorns and radar systems warned ships away, but the plane, high above it all, slipped with little fuss from international to sovereign territory and then, over the airport, began to circle lower.

No one knew she was back home and so, in a way, she wasn't. This was recess, free time, a life temporarily suspended. The tower blocks and office blocks and church spires of the city seemed to float in the evening air and for a moment her heart swelled to see all the windows, all the lives behind all the windows, and for a moment London felt like something splendid and stirring. It was cold but her rucksack wasn't heavy so instead of going directly home she decided to walk along the Thames towards London Bridge, a favourite stretch of river passing the concrete bulk of the Southbank Centre, the Tate Modern, Shakespeare's Globe. Behind her lay the Gothic masonry of the Houses of Parliament where the calm gold circle of the clock's face hung like a second moon.

Sometimes, at times like this, she was surprised by how long she'd been living in London. Seventeen years ago, when she and Janey had been teenagers sitting hot and bored on a sun-stunned summer lawn, they'd traced longing lines backwards from the outer suburbs across the pages of the A–Z into the heart of the city, where, Alice had been convinced, the important parts of life were happening. London was a place where she'd find conversations about things rather than people, a place where art and culture triumphed over the dull biology of suburban existence. Now every year she had to admit that it felt less and less like the imaginary city of her fervid teenage dreams.

Her phone buzzed with a text message from Callum inviting her to his next exhibition – an unsubtle bid for some free publicity in *Meta* – and wanting to know whether she'd found his checked shirt. Time reasserted itself. ('Women can't wait as long as men,' her mother had murmured when Alice and Callum broke up.)

Callum was one of those men of a certain haircut who

gravitated towards the east of the city. Just before the relationship had finally expired he'd been working on a series of sculptures about the alienation of the artist in society. Built from scrap metal and string and wood, they were ungainly, clattering things set in motion through a complicated system of pulleys and weights. Alice had helped him with the mechanics. One of the first happy thoughts she'd had after the split was that she'd no longer have to sit uncritically through his disquisitions on the nature of art. On his side she supposed that there would also have been relief. Callum had always complained that she could be cold, and that she over-intellectualized everything she did. Every time they watched a film, he said, she had to try to turn it into a college course. Sometimes, he said, a movie is just a dumb movie, end of story. Alice sympathized with him: it was true, for instance, that she had difficulties fully believing that an emotion was anything more than the little cracklings and sparkings of the synapses of her brain. She was never, as he said, fully *engaged*.

She put her phone away and continued walking towards London Bridge. The lights were coming on in the buildings and once more Alice felt excited. It was one of those unplanned, uncreatable moments when she felt absolutely right to be where she was, blissfully correct in her own life, in her anonymity among the crowds walking down by the Thames, watching here and there a secret light glowing through a window and briefly illuminating a table, a long beige corridor, a silent figure in a doorway. She was by a pub, the Three Roses, and she felt that the thing to do was to rush inside and order a whisky and sit in a window seat and eke out those last moments of her trip before she headed irrevocably back to her flat and before the feeling of rightness left her, as it quickly would do. She assumed that for some people (for her sister, she'd always suspected) the feeling of rightness came more often, stayed longer.

Her mobile buzzed again. 'Alice? It's Dayanita. So, babe, how was New York?'

'Hey,' said Alice, now wishing that she hadn't picked up. 'It was good, thanks. Ben from *Identify* says hello. I went to a knitting night.'

At some point, when Alice hadn't been paying attention, a world of domestic crafts – knitting, sewing, baking, jam-making – had become suddenly fashionable. Dayanita, who was *Meta*'s publicist, talked about joining the Women's Institute.

'Knitting? Sounds fun. It's ages since I was in New York. But listen, can you go on the radio tomorrow? It's a panel discussion about, er,' there was a rustling while Dayanita looked at her notes, 'the commodification of the nostalgic impulse?'

'Doesn't our beloved editor want to do it?'

'Tom's got a bad cold; he'll sound awful on the radio. Very phlegmy. Besides, you're our star critic. They want *you*. The car will be round at eight thirty? Okay? Damn. Got another call coming through that I have to take. Remember, eight thirty. Ciao, babe!'

Alice finished the whisky, the ice cubes bumping against her lips, and left the pub. At the cathedral she climbed a narrowly twisting staircase leading to the top of London Bridge. She had been to a service there once when she was a child taken to church every Sunday morning by her parents. She remembered watching them take Communion and a child's sense of outrage that they were kneeling before another adult, that they were being fed like babies or invalids. Later she'd gone to university and 'lost her faith' – an expression that she always felt implied an unfair carelessness. Lost, lapsed, apostate. Peter, who had been bought up Roman Catholic, used to laugh at Alice and tell her that she couldn't be a lapsed Protestant. 'That's like being a lapsed cinema-goer, a lapsed roller-skater,' he said. Alice thought her difficulties were with the communal aspect of organized religion. She'd always found the first-person plural problematic. 'I'm, you know, more a liminal sort of figure,' she said to Callum when he complained that she didn't spend enough time hanging out with his artist friends. 'A limin; like a lemming but less hairy.'

*

She boarded a bus headed east, to an area of unprettified canals and blockish concrete industrial units, and stopped where, in front of her building, two gasometers rose and fell incrementally, alternately revealing and obscuring the city beyond. Home, but the sort of home that, after four years, still felt like a temporary, precarious pitching point that would never provoke a strong feeling of return. Alice's unit was on the seventh floor of the block, and this she loved. Every morning familiar landmarks rose to greet her out of the city wash of glass and metal and concrete: the Millennium Dome, the thin Tower 42 building, the shining silver of Canary Wharf, a land-locked lighthouse with its blinking red warning. About a quarter of the units in the block had been turned semi-illegally into flats and the rest were still used by the trades: garment factories, wood and metal workshops, packaging outfits. The fag ends of a country that had almost stopped making things, the so-called Industrial Island Machine, the Pyramidal Workshop. Inside, her housemate, Isabel, was sitting wrapped in a sleeping bag – with its concrete floor and long row of single-glazed windows it was always cold in the unit. Isabel smelled very faintly, sourly, of alcohol and must have been partying all weekend because a flock of beer cans crowded around the bin, stragglers balanced on the windowsills. The remains of a Pot Noodle and three glass tumblers filled with red wine had been abandoned on the dining table.

'Darling, you're back! How was? How's Soph?' Isabel jumped up and hugged Alice quickly before going over to the stove. 'Tea? Builders? Peppermint? I feel absolutely rubbish – quite poisoned by drink. Oh, and you forgot to set up a new standing order before you went. The rent was due last week but I couldn't quite cover your half . . .' Isabel, a few years younger than Alice, lived on a mixture of furtive parental bank transfers and a growing number of brightly coloured credit cards. Her great-grandfather had been something quite important in India and her voice always made Alice think of the words 'high tea'. 'So how were the shows?' Isabel said.

Alice pulled a face. Mostly the art had seemed gaudy and smug and a little tired; engineered sensation with nothing much behind it. Nothing seeming to be at stake. A taxidermied stag had been hung halfway up the gallery wall from where it stared mournfully over the heads of the white-wine-drinking crowd. Reading her notes on the plane she'd thought that she wouldn't say any of that in the review, however, because the main artist was a friend of her editor.

'Enrico showed the stuffed stag thingy again,' she said. 'It was supposed to be the big piece but I can't think of anything to say about it. It had huge testicles. Like overgrown kiwi fruit. That's all I can remember. The huge testicles.' She sighed. Recently, writing anything seemed harder than it used to. Sometimes all she could find were the words of a playground chant repeated and repeated until they became nonsensical: Red lorry, yellow lorry, red lorry, yellow lorry, red lorry, yellow lorry, red lorry, yellow lorry, yellow.

She got up and dragged her rucksack into her bedroom, stretched and felt all the little bones in her neck click deliciously. Looking around, seeing the place with her tourist's eyes, she noticed how empty the room was without Callum's belongings. Why had she left it like that? With all the little spaces where a stereo had sat, a poster hung? Even the row of silver hooks on the back of the door retained a ghostly impression of his brown leather jacket and his long, black trench – the one he liked to wear with the collar turned up because it made him feel like a Russian spy. Alice pulled her own tweed jacket from off the end hook and hung it in the place where the black trench had swung. It felt like a small, pathetic victory.

'I bumped into Peter earlier,' Isabel called from the main room. 'He was talking about karaoke at the Prince George. And your mother rang.'

Recently there had been this awkward silence between them because Isabel wanted to move in with her boyfriend, Johnny. Or she wanted to move Johnny into the unit. And so Isabel and Alice had been circling around the problem of what to do with the flat, a discussion that was moving nowhere, that kept getting mired in the English compulsion for polite indirectness. Now, instead, Alice turned to her bag and pulled out a bottle of duty-free vodka. 'Look,' she said, 'presents! Will this make the hangover better or worse, do you think?'

Later, she tried to call her parents back, imagining the telephone handset with oversized red buttons – compensation for her father's failing eyesight – ringing on the small table in the hallway. There was no answer. Her mother had probably wanted to leave new instructions regarding their approaching trip: an eight-month world tour including two weeks in Australia staying with her father's cousin and then on to America to stay with her mother's younger sister, Carol, and her new husband. 'Our last fling,' her mother had said, giggling girlishly. Alice wasn't convinced that there'd ever been a first fling. Her mother had been acting strangely recently. 'Might as well blow some of our savings before the economy blows it for us,' her father had said, and such flippancy was quite out of character for him also. Several years earlier he'd retired from his job as a parks manager with the local council, and now it was as if he and her mother had suddenly decided to step out from behind the monumental forms they'd taken in Alice's childhood and show themselves as people – full of foibles and recklessnesses, and not at all godlike.

Alice replaced the receiver and went to look for something to eat in the cupboard. There were three tins of Spam brought home by Isabel several weeks earlier. 'It's recession chic,' she'd said. They hadn't eaten the Spam. It sat there alongside a tin of mandarin oranges and one of evaporated milk. War-baby food. Alice stared at the cans. Then she poured two large vodkas and rolled cigarettes. To avoid the jetlag she was trying to stay awake until at least eleven. Alice was bad with jetlag. She opened up her laptop and selected a track, listened for a while to something heavy and discordant but then, seeing Isabel's pained and hungover expression, exchanged it for an album of gentler, electronic seascapes.

Isabel took a swig of vodka and made a face but carried on drinking. 'Do you know what?' she said after a while. 'The vodka *is* making me feel better. The Swedish guys upstairs are having a party – shall we go?'

'A Tuesday party?'

'Tuesday is the new Thursday. Which means it's really Friday.' She shook what was left of the vodka bottle.

Alice thought briefly about the radio in the morning. 'Okay,' she said.

'It's fancy dress though.' Isabel looked around the unit and picked up a pair of sunglasses and her leather jacket. 'I'm going as a member of Baader–Meinhof.'

'You always go as a member of Baader–Meinhof.'

'So? It's easy. Come, Comrade Alice! Ve must to ze party!'

Alice shook her head. Isabel was bad with accents.

The familiar three o'clock, four o'clock terror was made up of a thousand little anxieties that massed into something imprecise, something not quite specific, something that might, perhaps, have been called death. Alice's mouth was dry from too much vodka and too many cigarettes. Her watch showed that there were just three more hours until she needed to get up for the radio show. The bearded neighbour lying next to her groaned in his sleep and rolled over. She glanced at him. *Oops*, she thought. *Whoops*.

To try to lull herself back to sleep she usually imagined running. She sat up and turned her pillow over so that fresh, cool cotton lay against her cheek. In her mind she built a sports arena with white lines stretching ahead over the dull, reddish surface of the oval track. There was a grey stand intimidatingly empty of spectators and a damp swatch of green grass, a familiar route traced out metre by metre, with herself placed inside it. Or not herself exactly but an avatar of sorts, dressed in shiny yellow viscose shorts. In real life Alice would never have worn shiny yellow viscose. She wasn't even sure what viscose was. Around her the imaginary air felt heavy, like an actual, tangible substance that she was powering inside as her feet picked up the rhythm – hit and lift, hit and lift – as though if she pumped her arms hard enough she'd rip the air apart and run straight through. In her head there was a voice, a word she couldn't understand, that came from somewhere deep within the grey stand, and she watched herself running, moving round and round the reddish track, round and round the damp greenness, round and round under the whitened cooling sky.

She slept, finally, somewhere towards dawn, until her alarm rang at seven thirty, rang again at seven forty-five, at eight. At five minutes past she threw herself under the shower before the water had had time to heat up and gulped coffee while looking for a pair of tights without a ladder. The Swede snored on; he'd have to find his own way out. In the taxi, on the way to the radio studio, she felt the underwire come out of the old bra picked up by mistake, the thin strip of metal digging into the flesh between her breasts. Outside it was raining, and the office workers with their black umbrellas moved like a Roman army in tortoise formation across the Hungerford Bridge. Each one was focused on the back of the one in front, none turning to look over to the thick, useless pillars of an older, abandoned bridge – empty little islands strung out across the Thames.

She sat in the studio smelling wet hair, damp clothes steaming gently in the heat. The show's presenter was talking – blah, blah, blah – and the other guest, a young academic, was saying something about the rise of the non-place – 'Marc Augé, of course, said . . .' – and then there was silence. Alice realized that she'd been asked a question but that she had no idea what it was. The silence grew. It was a live recording. She shifted in her seat trying to get the little piece of metal from her bra to move from where it was now pressed against her left breast. Her palms were sweaty. 'No?' she guessed. The presenter looked surprised. The young academic raised an eyebrow. 'Yes?' she tried. Her hand made a flapping movement on the table like a dying fish on the deck of a trawler somewhere far out in the North Sea. She felt as though she were trapped on a traffic island with the cars speeding by too quickly, the faces of the drivers and the passengers blurred, unrecognizable. Last night's vodka burned in her stomach. Alice wiped her palms against her trousers. 'Oh. Ah. I think I'm –' Then she leaned forward, grabbed the wastepaper bin and threw up.

To avoid going straight back to the office she walked through the now-thinning drizzle to Oxford Street to buy a new bra. She should offer to pay for the cleaning of the young academic's trousers. Oh God.

The assistant in the fitting room was short and sturdy with a faint moustache. She was a crusader, this woman, a bra missionary stranded in a country of heathens who failed to understand the importance of that vital female undergarment. 'Eighty per cent,' she said, 'eighty per cent of women in the UK are wearing the wrong-size bra.' She lectured Alice on drooping and sagging. She extolled the virtues of a good sports bra and demonstrated the foolishness of thin straps ('no support here or here'). Finally, rounding on her sternly, she grabbed the fastening of the cream bra Alice had been trying and pulled the material sharply on to the tightest setting. 'It's not about comfort!' the moustached woman barked. 'At your age, things drop, they go!'

Alice, feeling queerly powerless in her half-naked state, was relieved when a bell sounded from another cubicle and the woman left her alone in front of the mirror. She stared at her reflection. At her age? She considered the body in the glass. In the new, tighter bra her breasts were squeezed together and the thin skin between them was faintly creased, like crêpe paper. And wasn't it only the other day that she had noticed, quite suddenly, how much her hands had aged? They had become her mother's hands. The skin seemed thinner, crosshatched with tiny lines. Alice made a fist and saw bony knuckles. She spread out her fingers and saw prominent blue veins. It struck her that she might have been carrying her new hands around for years without noticing them. They didn't displease her but it was disconcerting nonetheless to find them attached to the ends of her arms, where she remembered a pair of girl's hands residing.

She paid for the new bras and walked (the rain had finally ended) to the tube stop. Perhaps she had just missed a train, perhaps it was the office hour, but strangely, most unusually, there was no one else in the ticket hall and the heavy metal teeth of the escalators, engaged in their separate Sisyphean journeys, were loud in the fluorescent silence. Down on the platform there was a poster advertising a new pill to combat *Daily Fatigue Syndrome*. 'Daily Fatigue Syndrome? Isn't that, like, living? Isn't that life?' said Alice to the small mouse that was nosing around the rails. Alice had a soft spot for tube mice, the little animated balls of black fluff. Peter had once told her that they lived off the flakes of human skin that collected on the tube tracks, but she'd decided not to hold that against them.

Trying to work out who might have heard the broadcast, she crept shakily past *Meta*'s receptionist and went to the bathroom, where she splashed water on her face, thinking, *Even this will pass away*. It wasn't really a comfort. Dayanita came in. 'Alice!' she said. 'What was that? What were you *doing*?' Alice fled shamefaced towards her desk. Peter, who sat next to her and whom she sometimes felt as though she'd known for ever, waved and made a gagging sound. She switched on her monitor and scrolled through her emails. Something from one of the newspapers she occasionally wrote for, asking if she'd cover a feature on the forthcoming Dorothea Lange retrospective. Around her, the walls of the office were nicotine-stained from before the smoking ban and there were patches of creeping damp near the ceiling. A poster for a French philosophical symposium hung apathetically next to her desk, looking as if it might, at any moment, give up its tenuous hold and slide to the floor. Rumours about the future of the magazine – the lack of a future – were thick and constant. Advertising was down and certain key investors, suddenly nervous for their personal finances, were withdrawing funding. 'I'm just not convinced of the urgency of this project any more,' one of them had said before leaving. 'I just feel we need to be pulling together instead of picking things apart.'

Privately, Alice was in any case feeling increasingly sceptical about *Meta*'s relevance. She had spent too many depressing hours wrestling with the works of the sorts of academics favoured by the editor, and reformulating them for *Meta*'s readership. Sexing up the academic prose; taking delicately scalpelled thoughts and translating them into blunt cudgels. 'Sometimes,' Alice said to Peter, 'I look down at my desk and it's a time warp there. It's still 1968. 1976 on a good day. It's all Lacan and prawn cocktails and Black Forest gateau.' At endless meetings the editor *talked* about revitalizing the pages, about the necessity of engaging with the changing times. 'Yes, but I wonder,' he said when Alice once suggested a piece on the factories of China, 'whether we shouldn't commission an article on the history of the grooming of pubic hair.' Ever since 9/11 *Meta's* now-unfortunate subhead – 'International Intellectual Cultural Terrorism' – had crept into smaller and smaller fonts before finally sliding quietly off the glossy front cover. Given production costs, the fact that the front cover remained glossy at all was a small monthly miracle.

As the day went on, Alice noticed how unsettled the office had become, much worse now than before her trip: everyone talking in low voices behind closed doors, little groups congregating in the kitchen, by the cloakroom, and then drifting away as soon as someone else walked by. It was difficult to concentrate on any proper work. Peter was eating a banana. 'Do you think,' Alice said, 'that the banana is an inherently comic fruit? If you were born in a country where bananas had always existed – where *is* the banana indigenous? – would you still find them funny?' Peter shook his head. He didn't know about bananas. She no longer felt sick and sweaty but was tired and wanted something salty to eat. Unholy bleeps and occasional electronic screams were coming from the desk of Theo, the magazine's editorial assistant and games reviewer, who was busy trafficking central European prostitutes in some bleak industrial cityscape.

'Theo,' Alice said, 'did you organize the contracts filing cabinet while I was away?'

Theo looked up. 'Err, no.' He was silent for a moment and then he sighed. Theo's sighs were eloquent: this one contained forbearance, resignation and the suggestion that Alice had asked him to undertake some entirely unreasonable task quite beneath his job description. 'Shall I do it now?'

Alice sighed in turn, but hers, she felt, was a disappointingly vacant expulsion of air. 'No, don't worry about it.'

The editor strode by looking harassed, making for the sanctuary of his little room at the back of the office. 'Alice, welcome back. Looking forward to hearing about New York. Ah, Theo, can you come through in five? Want to brainstorm a few things with you . . .'

'Absolutely,' said Theo, grinning. Theo, Alice suspected, would do well. He knew how to pick and choose from the tasks assigned to him. She tried to remember whether she'd been as irritating as a 22-year-old, but the past is not just a foreign country, it is a remote enisled land within shark-infested waters and shrouded, often, with a sea mist. It is hard to find a trusted pilot or skipper to take you there.

Alice turned back to the pile of papers on her desk, wondering what had happened to the dream of the paperless office. Claire, the magazine's managing editor, looked up from her production corner where a flat-plan of the next issue was taped to the wall and sets of corrected proofs sat in neat piles. 'Alice,' she said, 'I need your New York piece. End of the day tomorrow?' Alice nodded. She still hadn't thought of anything to say about the show. Red lorry, yellow lorry, red lorry, yellow lorry, red lorry, yellow lorry, red lorry, yellow lorry, yellow. She turned and opened the window by her desk and felt, quite distinctly, a cold strip of air flowing through the warm like cool cream poured over steaming custard on a Christmas pudding.

By six o' clock it was dark outside and a frieze of fat, horrific pigeons hopped and shuffled on mutilated claws along the edge of the roof of the opposite building.

'See you at the pub?' said Peter, heading out of the door.

Alice nodded. She wondered how long Anka would last. Secretly Alice thought of Peter as her romantic backstop, someone who could be relied upon for cinema trips and last-minute dinner dates. She'd always had a vague idea that if they both reached forty and found themselves single (a time which no longer felt inconceivably far away) they'd give in and set up house together. She liked that he could recite, with appropriate voices, the entire Christmas dinner scene from Ingmar Bergman's *Fanny and Alexander*. Her mobile bleeped. She still hadn't managed to speak to her parents. 'Where does all the time go?' she and her other childless, semi-employed friends regularly groaned. 'How can we get anything done?' *It's because I don't drive*, Alice said. *It's because everything takes longer in London.*

Isabel and Peter were sitting in a booth at the back of the pub. Isabel waved Alice over. 'Oh God, Alice, I heard. How awful.'

'I think I may need to change career.'

'Come have a seat.' Isabel stood up and kissed her on the cheek. 'Let me get you a drink.'

Alice slid into the booth opposite Peter. He was reading a magazine and she craned her neck to try and see the standfirst.

Peter looked up and flipped the page: 'It's about humans having an over-developed sense of cause and effect, something that primes us to see design and purpose in everything.' He put down the magazine. 'According to this study, even people who describe themselves as atheists or agnostics often tacitly attribute purpose to traumatic events – they still see some sort of outside agency.'

Alice nodded. She was watching Isabel at the bar talking to a stooping boy wearing a lumberjack shirt. People's faces were splashed with little lights from the disco ball, silvered shapes that swam across their skin like shoals of ghost fish somewhere deep and unknown in the middle of the ocean. She was thinking also, *Why couldn't they? Why did it never seem to be the right moment to change what she felt into something that could be called a relationship?*

Peter's phone beeped with a message. He looked at it. 'Oh,' he said. And then, 'Ah.' And then, 'You should check your phone too. It's sort of about a change of career . . .'

Alice groaned. 'I knew Tom looked more stressed today.' *And then perhaps it was because she always felt that she already had, and that sometimes when she looked at him it was as if they'd already lived a whole life together, got married, had children and grown old and there was nothing else to say.*

Peter nodded. He stood up. 'Izzy! We want Scotch. We want, uh, lots and lots of alcoholic drink.' He waved a twenty-pound note. Alice took out her compact mirror and surreptitiously rubbed more blusher on to her pale, hungover cheeks.

The next morning Alice and Peter stood with cardboard boxes at their respective desks and considered five years' worth of accumulated office ephemera. 'Maybe we should wait to see whether things start up again,' said Alice. *Meta* was suspending operations – suspending, not closing, the editor said, but suspending without pay. There was a rumour he was considering a job at a publishing house.

Peter picked up one of his snow globes – he collected snow globes – and shook it in her face. 'Risky. We may never get back into the offices again, and there's my pension in here somewhere. I'm assured of it.' He gulped from the bottle of wine they'd found abandoned in the kitchen and passed it to Alice, who was shovelling a pile of CDs into one of her boxes.

'Oh look, CDs!' said Peter. 'How quaint!'

Alice ignored him and bent down to pull her Karin Ericsson print from out behind her desk. She dusted off the glass. Despite many successes – Ericsson had exhibited with everyone, been name-checked by successive generations of younger artists – she'd never quite made the leap into the consciousness of the general public. Several years ago, following her major *Sakhalin* exhibition in Paris and the moment when Alice had been convinced that Ericsson was about to go stratospheric – napkin-signing famous – she'd abruptly retired, issuing a statement to the press and quietly disappearing. Alice's picture, from the 1969 'Sea-Struck' series, was a stormy-looking black offset print on white lightweight cardboard. She'd bought it at auction – 'Sea-Struck' was considered a minor series and had still been affordable at the time.

'Look,' she said to Peter. 'A year and a half that's been here. I'm too disorganized. I shouldn't be allowed to own art.'

She picked up her address book: pages of hard-won contacts, but she knew that being on the staff at *Meta* had made her lazy, that she'd let certain freelance commissions slide at just the moment when, disillusioned as she was becoming with the magazine, she should have been throwing herself at other London editors. But then she wasn't sure that it was just *Meta* she was losing interest in. 'I've run out of superlatives,' she'd said to Peter after failing to file a piece of copy. 'Don't you ever worry that our period, artistically speaking, is going to be one of those dull, end-of-era moments that historians skip over in order to get to the exciting new thing? I think we're going to be massively skipped.' For a time all her articles managed eventually to come to some variation on that point. 'Or maybe it's just me,' she'd said. 'Maybe it's a personal thing.' Peter had nodded. 'Perhaps you just need to write about something else,' he'd said. 'You should get into politics. Or travel writing.'

Dayanita walked into the room trailing a ball of wool and speaking into her mobile. Her eyes looked red. She got off the phone and came over to Alice and Peter.

'It's just all so *sad*. It just doesn't seem real yet.' She dropped her ball of wool on to Alice's desk and reached forwards and Alice submitted uncomfortably to a hug. 'I keep thinking of all the good times,' said Dayanita damply into Alice's shoulder. 'We've got to stay in touch though, okay?' (Alice remembered the first time she'd met Dayanita, who'd evaded her proffered hand with a cry of 'No, no, I'm a huggy person,' and lunged. 'I'm a kind of repressed personal-space freak,' Alice had said into the air to the left of Dayanita's ear.) Dayanita stepped back and gave her a watery smile. She made a little clenched fist and sort of bopped Alice's hand before turning to Peter. Alice raised her eyebrows at him and drank some more of the wine (it wasn't bad). Her mobile rang.

'Alice! I feel as though it's been months since we spoke. How *are* you?'

'Oh . . .' Alice glanced around at the half-stripped office. 'Hi, Mum. Everything's, you know, it's all good.'

'Now, Alice, are you sure you're all right? We just read about your magazine in the paper. What are you going to do?'

'Ah, yes, the magazine. I didn't realize it had made the news . . .' Alice rubbed her stomach; there was a pain in her gut. 'I expect I'll do some more freelance work; just wait for a bit and see what happens. The closure's not definite at this point. We might start up again.'

She'd hoped to avoid this particular conversation, seeing in advance how it would play out. *Freelance? What about job security, Alice? What about a pension? How will you get a mortgage if you're just working freelance contracts?* And every time she visited her parents, this 'freelance' and what her mother viewed as Alice's somewhat directionless life would be the elephant in the room, sitting next to her in the space on the oatmeal sofa that used to be Janey's and snuffling at the tea tray, at the home-made chocolate cake, with its long trunk, the tip like a little questing hand, like an entire other creature swinging from the front of the elephant's face. In the years since Janey had gone, in the time since Alice had moved to the city, Alice's relationship with her parents seemed to have dwindled to these tea trays, to roast dinners and Victoria sponges, to a sort of peaceful distance, tinged occasionally with a regret that it was so. Love measured out in cakes: pink and white birthday sponges; heavy, fruit-filled Christmas cakes; Easter simnel cakes decorated with eleven marzipan Apostles.

Her mother was talking again: 'Why don't you come home for a bit, save on all that rent you pay in London until you find another proper job? You'd be doing us a favour really because we don't have anyone to look after the house while we're away, water the garden when it gets warmer. Dad's fretting about his plants.'

'Gosh, Mum, it's good of you to offer but –'

'You don't have to make a decision now, just have a chat with Isabel and get back to us. It seems silly, the house standing empty and you paying out for that . . . place.' Her mother had never been very keen on the unit. 'And it really would be a comfort to think that someone's keeping everything ticking over while we're gone . . . Imagine if the pipes burst again – it's been so cold this winter, icy. Mrs Austin slipped in the alley at the top of the road last week. Did I tell you that? She broke her hip and had to go into, you remember the old people's home near the park? The Lighthouse? She's there convalescing if you have a chance to visit . . .'

They talked some more, mainly about people Alice no longer really knew, and then, because Peter was making impatient faces at her, Alice said she had to go.

'I'm finished,' said Peter. 'Let's share a taxi, dump the stuff at mine and then go to the Prince George.'

Alice nodded. She was thinking about Mrs Austin and feeling badly because it had been a long time since they'd spoken. Mrs Austin, who'd once been her Girl Guide leader, was responsible for Alice's ability to light a campfire with a single match, recite, in order, the books of the Old Testament and orientate a map. Also, she lived on the same street as Alice's parents and in the first months after Janey's disappearance Mrs Austin had come to be one of the few people Alice could bear to talk to, one of the few whose opinions and condolences didn't set her teeth on edge. She really should visit Mrs Austin. Alice took out her compact and redid her lipstick. New York Red. Chanel. 'Will you book a cab, Peter, or shall we look for one outside?' She put away the lipstick and grimaced. 'I'm really going to miss expense accounts.'

At the Prince George it was the end of the winter party season and there were several loud groups of office workers. 'Amateur drunks,' whispered Peter. They joined Johnny and Isabel sitting drinking pints of lager at one of the long, sticky tables facing the bar. The Prince George, in a probably doomed attempt to remain a working-class, East End pub, avoided real-ale pumps and Belgian beers.

'When are we going to get bored of this?' said Alice.

'Of what?' said Johnny, palming peanuts from their little foil bag into his mouth.

'Oh, I don't know. Of not doing anything useful. Whatever. You know, doctoring like Sophie or teaching or social work. Imagine if everyone here walked out and got a proper job.'

'Just because you comment on a problem doesn't mean you're not a part of it,' said Peter.

Alice ignored him. 'Isabel? Are you going to the bar? Will you get me a pint?'

Someone was singing 'My Way'. They'd forgotten that it was karaoke night, switched from a Saturday in an effort to shake off some of the art students who had taken to loudly monopolizing the singing and annoying the regulars. The policy hadn't been entirely successful. Anka arrived late from an MA private view, and she and Peter danced. Alice turned to Isabel. 'But she's so *young*. What do they talk about? Why doesn't she find some friends her own age to play with?'

'Hey,' said Isabel, 'you shouldn't let their relationship, shallow and superficial as it may be, become emblematic of a patriarchal society which favours the younger woman and starts looking to cast you on to the scrap heap as you near the end of your childbearing potential.'

'Oh God,' said Alice, 'you do say the nicest things.'

A boy wearing a First World War flying hat came up to their table. 'Alice! Izzy!' He leaned over and kissed their cheeks. 'Alice, I've been hearing all about your radio thing! What *happened*?'

(Just sometimes Alice thought that she'd stayed too long at the party. It was as if she'd gone to the bar for a drink and, from politeness, got caught talking to someone she wasn't really interested in, and by the time she escaped the people she wanted to be with had left and there were sad, sticky patches of spilled drinks on the floor.)

Official closing time came and went, and the evening was reaching that point where no one stayed on who hadn't given up on the idea of the following morning. The office workers had left. Johnny and Isabel had vanished. Anka had gone home because she had to be up early for her part-time job in a coffee bar. Stumbling, Alice and Peter went out on to the street to smoke and stare in the window of the new shop (formerly a wholesale clothing company) selling second-hand clothes and bric-a-brac. The owners had replaced the old plastic sign with a newly faded wooden board: *J. K. Goldstein Food* in peeling gold letters. Through the door of the Prince George leaked the sounds of Blondie, and Alice swayed gently on the spot like a cut-out paper doll, trying hard to focus on Peter. He *was* good-looking, she thought. She changed her mind about that all the time. Recently he'd grown a moustache and it quite suited him. He looked like a character from an American indie movie and his shoes had little tassels on them. *Loafers*, thought Alice and was then inordinately pleased with her powers of observation and recall. Peter was looking up now at the stars trying (he never succeeded) to make out the Plough, tracing the shape with his finger like a child learning to read.

'Art,' said Alice thoughtfully, 'can be divided into work which is a window on to the world and work which *is* the world.' She hiccoughed. 'Peter. Important question for you. Peter, are you happy?'

'Yes,' said Peter, and he gave a little whoop to prove it. Alice grinned and whooped back. The future loomed ominous but that thought seemed far away, glimpsed harmlessly through a fine gauze of white lines.

'I'm going to work for my brother,' said Peter. 'He runs a little business selling essays to students at his university. A not inconsiderable percentage of the philosophy department will graduate only

28

because of him.' Peter, unlike Alice, had never been described as one of London's 'trendiest young cultural critics'. Peter had no great expectations for his freelance career. 'I'll be educating myself in all those fascinating courses I never took – Freud as a modernist text; media law; social geography.'

Alice brushed her hair back and said she was thinking of moving out to the suburbs for a while and letting Isabel and Johnny take over the unit.

'Oh, Alice!' said Peter.

'Besides I just can't bear to job-hunt and pitch ideas around right now. I can't bear to ring up the newspaper editors and sit through the obligatory snuffling about, you know, the radio incident. Even if they don't say anything I'll still know that they're *snuffling*.'

'Yes, but Alice, really, what will you *do* out there?' he said, making it sound as though she were moving to the middle of the moors, to John o'Groats, Land's End.

Alice pushed away the memory of the oppressive order and neatness of her parents' house. The feeling, always, of Sunday afternoon. The scents of furniture polish and bleach. 'Hide my shame. Develop an unhealthy interest in cats. Write a Hollywood screenplay . . . Anyway, will you miss me terribly? Will you pine?' She poked him in the stomach. The beer was making everything woozy but was still cut through here and there by flashes of sharpness. Peter gave a sad little whoop and offered her a cigarette. She was smoking a roll-up but took it anyway.

'You know I don't want you to go,' said Peter.

She stared at him. The stars glimmered as best they could through the light pollution. Peter blew a smoke ring.

She reached out and gripped hold of him for balance.

The gasometer had risen to its fullest extent, hiding a cylindrical-shaped portion of the city from Alice's view. Somewhere between her sleeping and waking the snow had come in great gusts, banking all around like a childhood dream. From the draughty window she watched a girl with bright red hair cycling along by the canal, a green scarf wrapped around her throat and streaming out behind her as she travelled past the yellow-brick Victorian church (converted now into flats) and on into the early morning distance. Alice felt cold and sick with drink, and her chest was tight from too many cigarettes. She got up, sniffing, and quickly pulled on as many clothes as possible. Peter must have left some time during the night.

In the kitchen she switched on the radio. Across the capital and out into the suburbs buses and trains had ground to a halt, schools and offices were closed. She could see through the window that already a lumpen snowman had sprouted just beyond the gate to the yard. The papers reported a shortage of salt to grit the roads; panic-buying in the supermarkets; stranded cars on the motorways. It was a long time since the South-East had felt so *elemental*. 'It's unnatural,' said a woman to the radio presenter. 'It's global warming.'

'First the money and now this,' said Isabel, when she appeared in search of coffee. 'Do you think the apocalypse is coming? Did Peter stay over last night?'

'We're out of coffee,' said Alice. 'There's tea in the pot.' She and Isabel were too disorganized, always running out of whatever they needed and ending up washing the dishes with cheap shampoo, their hair with even cheaper washing-up liquid. She opened the door on to the narrow concrete walkway and poked her head outside. There was a clean frostiness that even the London city fug couldn't disguise. The fresh air slapped at her and Alice's stomach heaved.

Last night, after finally falling asleep, she'd dreamed that she was lying in her bed sleeping and in her dream had woken up, lain awake a while and then fallen back to sleep again. More and more she'd been dreaming like this – and waking in the morning unable to remember which hours of the night she'd really been asleep and which hours conscious. It was as if her imagination had emptied itself out.

She closed the door and retreated back to the warmth of the flat.

Part Two

'Plunge in boldly and look to the object you are trying to attain, and don't bother about your own safety.'

How Girls Can Help to Build Up the Empire: The Handbook for Girl Guides
(1912)

When Alice and Janey were girls they lived at the edges of the *A–Z*, out where each page was covered with pale green quadrants and blocks of white and scatterings of pinkly beige triangles the colour of Elastoplast, and where two golden A roads cut across the squares of the map and ran along the bottom of a golf course and clipped the edges of a small wood. It always seemed a little fantastical to them that the thin white road where they lived really existed on something as official and impersonal as the *London A–Z*.

From their front garden they could see the green-tinted tower blocks in town rising out of a hazy blueness, and in the opposite direction, behind the house, were the woods, which stretched into an area of heathland decorated with an improbable clump of Scots pines – introduced, their father said, because of a nineteenth-century enthusiasm for the Scottish Highlands. (When Alice was a girl her father seemed to know everything. Later, when she was studying for her A-level examinations and beginning to realize that he didn't, she had felt obscurely cheated in some way.) There was a path through the woods named Baker Boy Lane because, as children whispered in the playground, a baker's boy, cutting through the green, had been murdered there, or had got lost, or had disappeared. They built tree houses and sat high up in the branches of the oak and ash and sweet chestnut with the thin green scent of nettles all around them. When it snowed they played Scott of the Antarctic, taking it in turns to be poor, snow-blind Captain Oates waving goodbye at the doorway of the tent. 'I'm just going out,' said Janey, 'I may be some time.'

In Alice's memory their Tudorbethan house was always filled

with the certainties of their mother's baking, the quiet industry of their father's interminable gardening and home improvements. There were the endlessly repeated rhythms of each week: church on a Sunday, piano lessons on a Monday, Girl Guides on a Wednesday evening in the draughty prefab hut next to the library. Over the doorway of the hut was a painting of brown-blond Jesus with his pale hand resting on the shoulder of a blue-uniformed Guide. He looked slightly creepy in that picture, like the sort of hip young teacher who played guitar and was into jazz and really 'got' the kids but turned out, years later, to have been a molester of some sort.

Alice had rented a car to move her clothes and books down from London. (Her father's Rover sat quietly in the garage: it would have pained him too much to think of someone else in the driving seat.) Her furniture, the little she'd amassed, stayed in the unit with Isabel: there wasn't much storage space in her parents' semi-detached with the three bedrooms which had never, when Alice was a teenager, seemed far enough away from one another. She'd stood in the porch fumbling for her keys and had glimpsed through the bay window the decorative plates that formed a grid across the Anaglypta wallpaper, the light reflected off the brass companion set that stood by the gas fire. Everything neat and in its place. She'd fought an urge to turn away and climb back into the rental car.

Now, several weeks later, she was lying in bed and hearing the still-unfamiliar gurgling of the central heating as she watched several sparrows dart and spin in front of the bedroom window. How lovely to wake up in a room that registered somewhere above freezing, to poke your toes out on to a soft carpet. Little pleasures. Downstairs in the hallway the barometer read, as always, 'changeable', though Alice tapped it hopefully with one finger as she passed, willing the thin metal arrow to spin around on its axis and take them to some more exciting weather front. *Very dry* was written on the barometer in curly Gothic script. *Stormy*. But the arrow never moved that far to the left or right. In the dining room she opened the French windows and watched as a single blackbird landed on the lawn, hopped around the flowerless hydrangeas. Her father's garden was always scrupulously maintained – a credit to the Parks Department – each successive year unfolding steadily, progressing properly and promptly, from trenches dug in January to the first mowing in April, watering and pruning in August, compost in November.

In London, Alice thought, she'd forgotten the silences of the suburbs. The way that out here a siren was a real, specific disaster rather than a general aural backdrop. Now sound came to her in distinct layers. The branches of the single apple tree rustling overhead, jostled briefly by a plump wood pigeon; a single car labouring up the hill; and far away the lazy sound of an aeroplane slicing through the sky. Years ago there had been more trees; not just apple but also plum and pear – stunted, diseased trees with wonderfully low branches that were easy for small girls to climb. She and Janey had cried when their father took a saw to the last plum tree, having campaigned unsuccessfully for a reprieve. How fiercely she'd been attached to everything in the garden, reactionary and territorial in the way that small children are and loving it all less for what it was than because it was hers. A sudden desolate feeling brimmed inside her and she turned hurriedly away.

Coming home now Alice found herself continually ambushed by these memories of her sister. Inside the house, walking through a particular doorway into a flat slab of sunshine, or just raising her arm and seeing flesh at a certain angle against a familiar wall, the past seventeen years would dissolve vertiginously away and she would expect again to hear Janey's voice, high and low, calling her from some other room, some next-door place.

Her mobile bubbled but she let it ring out and then listened to the message. 'Alice? It's Carla here. Heard about *Meta* – bloody shame – wondered if that meant you were free to write something for us? Do ring. And don't worry about the radio thing. We've all completely forgotten about it already.' Alice switched off the phone and shook her head. The growing suspicion that she had nothing to say, nothing to say it with, had clung to her all the way down from London like the stench of fried meat or the fug of yesterday evening's cigarettes. The last thing she wanted was a piece to write. She still had some savings and for extra cash – cash in hand – she was producing essays for failing university students. ('But you don't need to do that, Alice,' said Peter, when she called him to ask for his brother's phone number. 'Everyone wants you to write for them.' She hadn't tried to explain.)

Upstairs she hunched over her old school desk. Ah, virginal girl-hood bedroom! Cheap, varnished pine the colour of butter and sugar melted in a pan. The wallpaper a mass of clouds in pastel pink, lavender, blue. On the small shelf above the bed her childhood encapsulated in books: *The Famous Five* and *Narnia*, then *Z for Zachariah*, an ink-stained French pocket dictionary and *Lord of the Flies*. Her white confirmation Bible (Revised Standard Edition) and her old Girl Guide handbook. Pinned to a cork noticeboard a photograph of Alice and Janey crouched over a rock pool with their hair all wind-whipped, salt-thickened, blown together so that Janey became dark and Alice fair. Janey in the picture always smiling and laughing, always convinced that everybody loved her and so everybody always did. Janey was the sort of girl who would suddenly start dating the boy you'd secretly nursed a crush on for the past year but then do it so charmingly that you'd end up liking her even more.

Despite, perhaps because of, the silence Alice was finding it diffi-cult to concentrate, found it strange that she couldn't just wander out of her room and see Isabel sitting with her small silver laptop and humming as she uploaded images from her camera. Trying to type felt like pushing her fingers through green jelly. Her mind wan-dered: she still hadn't been to visit Mrs Austin at the nursing home. Did they have visiting hours like a hospital? Did you need to make an appointment? This was the sort of thing a reasonable adult should know, she thought. She got up and unwrapped the 'Sea-Struck' print she'd brought with her from London, propped it up at the back of her dressing table and stared at it for a while – the upside-down clouds and the stormy water. The leaves of the apple tree rustled. Janey sitting among the lower branches swinging suntanned legs and laughing through the bedroom window.

'Oh, just get lost why don't you,' said Alice, pushing her fingers determinedly through two more sentences of jelly.

The house phone rang and when she went to pick it up the display showed her old London number. Alice imagined Isabel scrunched up on the sofa holding their insouciantly old-fashioned cream telephone, the dial that turned with an analogue whirr and bruised the tips of your fingers.

'But listen,' she said, 'I have a favour to ask you. Last week we went to a warehouse party and found the cutest dog that had been left just tied up in the yard outside. The poor thing was nearly crazed with hunger and thirst and no one seems to know who it belongs to.' Isabel had been brought up with pets. To her, every animal was a friend she had yet to meet. To Alice every animal was a potential rabid savage. Of the two sisters it had been Janey who liked dogs and used to throw sticks for the big slobbering hounds being walked in the woods behind their house.

'Anyway,' Isabel continued, 'clearly he'd been abandoned and so we rescued him. And now we don't know what to do. I mean, he's a big dog – gorgeous temperament, but he's not a *city* dog, if you see what I mean. I'm going to ask my parents if they'll take him, but they're in the Bahamas for the winter. My mother's arthritis. And Peter can't have it at his place because of the landlord. And Johnny and I are going to be in Vienna a lot for Johnny's residency and, like I said, he's not really a city animal . . .'

'You want to bring the dog here, are you saying?' Alice could almost hear Isabel's disingenuous shrug. 'But Izzy, you know I don't *like* dogs. I cross the pavement to avoid them sometimes. They scare me with all those teeth and that weird alienness of their eyes. It's freaky.'

Isabel made an impatient noise with her teeth. 'It's not for ever. Just until my parents get back. If we take him to the RSPCA you know he'll be put down. I couldn't bear it. He *trusts* us. We rescued him. Besides, you keep complaining about how bored you are down there. How you have nothing to do?'

'Okay,' said Alice. 'But this is temporary, right? Just until your parents come home.'

'Oh Alice,' said Isabel, 'I knew we could rely on you! Peter and I will bring him down as soon as possible. I'm flying to Vienna tonight to see Johnny so I've put the puppy in kennels, but I'll bring him just as soon as I'm back.'

'Okay, sure. And tell Johnny lots of congratulations from me. And come soon to visit, okay? Come when you're back.'

She replaced the receiver and wandered aimlessly into her parents' bedroom. The respective sides of the double bed – his side, her side – were little islands of unknowability. A blood donor card marked the place in her mother's Catherine Cookson novel. On her father's side a selection of bottles and blister packs of pills (for high blood pressure, for rheumatism) stood next to a small blue Bible. The childhood tiptoeing around her father, who never expressed his wishes in words but through certain emanations, depressions and headaches, around which the women learned to navigate. 'Your parents rather terrify me,' Callum had whispered the first time Alice had taken him home. 'They're so 1950s.' It troubled her father that all of life could not be arranged as neatly as his municipal parks. That men in uniform would not uphold his directives in the family home and would not stop his younger daughter Janey, who'd again been banned from going out one evening, from regarding him scornfully across the table and slowly – it was insolence, wasn't it? – laying her knife and fork neatly to one side of her untasted plate.

From the window you could look down and see, ranging right and left, the long strips of back gardens: rockeries, rose bushes, washing lines, lawns scuffed by footballs and lawns neatly maintained in darker and paler stripes. The neighbours' teenage son, Daniel, Danny, was poking around the flowerbeds. He'd grown taller since she'd last seen him but there was still, she'd always thought it, something strangely blank about his face; something that half made you want to slap his cheek just to see the expression change. He stopped and looked up suddenly, staring directly at the window where Alice stood. She didn't think, from that angle, that he could see her, but she waved anyway, feeling that she was intruding on a private moment.

In the shower she let too-hot water sluice over her skull and then was towelling herself dry – soft towels in white and beige and mint, unlike the hard, scratchy, threadbare things she and Isabel kept – when the phone rang for a second time. *Just like a horror movie*, said Janey cheerfully. Alice wrapped the towel around her chest and walked damply back downstairs, stared at the caller's number. Every time this happened, an unfamiliar number, there was a thought that it might be her sister. Even now. What would she say? The transiently intolerable disappointment when the caller who was never Janey spoke. She picked up the phone.

'Alice?' It was her mother in America, sounding thin and far away.

'Hi there, *Mom*,' said Alice.

'Are you well? How's the house? Do you remember to turn the heating off at night? Fuel prices are terrible at the moment.'

'Yes,' said Alice, 'yes, I remember to turn the heating off at night. So how was Australia?'

Her mother sighed comfortably. 'Oh, well, it was lovely of course but so hot. Too hot for me. I mean you can't really enjoy yourself in that heat. And then the hotel we stayed at, there were a lot of those, you know, those *men*. With no wives. It makes your father uncomfortable . . . But it's really lovely here at Carol's. Did I tell you that she's got five bedrooms? They bought it when the housing market crashed, and the views from her porch are quite wonderful. Now, I just wanted to say that you must remember to be careful if you go up to London because the city's on red alert again for one of those terrorist attacks. I saw it on the news.'

'Sure. Yup.' Alice grabbed a handful of wet hair and squeezed it so that drops of water darkened the hall carpet.

'Sometimes, Alice, I don't think you realize how precious life is. Anyway, I wanted to talk to you about your cousin. Carol is ever so worried about her. She's been so moody recently. Terribly down. And,' her mother's voice dropped, 'she's not getting on well with Carol's new husband. We thought a change of scenery might help. Emily's never been to Europe. We thought she could come over and stay with you at our house for a bit.'

'Mu-um. I'm sort of busy . . .'

'Yes darling, but Emily isn't a baby, she's sixteen. She won't need looking after all the time. And it will give Carol a chance to have a proper honeymoon with Larry.'

'Aren't I too irresponsible?'

Her mother laughed. 'I'll talk to Carol about dates. It's going to be a wonderful opportunity for Emily.'

Alice put the phone down, shaking her head at her mother's terrible idea. She barely remembered Carol from before she emigrated; recalled, mostly, her jewellery. Carol was never without a pair of earrings, whether modestly expensive pearl studs or huge, cheaply flamboyant hoops; looping trails of beads; a silver charm bracelet that rattled as she lifted a teacup to her lipsticked mouth. Alice had never met Emily but she'd seen the photographs, the show reels, the modelling assignments stretching back to when Emily had been a blonde-haired, blue-eyed toddler. There had been a lot of catalogue work – she was too short, too preppy-looking for the catwalk – and, a year ago, a television commercial for some sort of breakfast cereal. Alice had watched the advert online. Emily's large eyes were surprisingly vacant, which, combined with the constantly parted pink-frosted lips, gave her the perpetual air of someone who had just been hit over the head with a large, blunt object.

At the Lighthouse Nursing Home the carpet muffled the footsteps of the white-uniformed nurse who moved forwards to welcome Alice and write her name in the large, spiral-bound visitors book. They walked down a long corridor, now and then passing silently shuffling men and women. Each one wore the confused expression of a child who had gone alone to visit the lighthouse, climbed the vertiginous steps inside the white tower and come to the room at the top from where the light shines out and from where they were now watching their companions down below, out in the sunshine, building sandcastles, talking, laughing, but very small, very distant, their words lost in the air.

The nurse, whose whiteness glimmered in the shadowy corridor, pushed open a pair of fire-retardant doors and a smell of cooked food blossomed. Alice saw rows of unframed pencil drawings and watercolours hung from the walls; still lives worked in charcoal and pastel and chalk.

'I see you're admiring our little gallery,' said the nurse, smoothing back her hair in its neat bun. 'Everything here is the residents' work – the dementia cases.' She rearranged the small gold cross that hung from a chain around her neck. 'You're not aware, I suppose, that with the onset of dementia a person often goes through an intensely creative stage: drawing, sewing, painting and so forth. We had a specialist in just the other week, a student doing casework, who explained that it's all linked to the loss of the language faculty somehow.'

Alice stopped in front of a charcoal drawing of a bunch of long-stemmed roses in a tall vase. The flowers were rather good, she thought.

'Oliver painted that last year. He could hardly speak by then, but his paintings (to my mind and I'm no expert) just seemed to get better and better. He would spend hours painting. He would have painted all day if we'd let him. Peculiar; a person who's never even picked up a paintbrush before can be overtaken by this compulsion. I often think it's as if they're trying to communicate some thought, some message, before everything disappears for good.'

'Did he . . . pass away?'

'No, no; he just moved beyond that stage. You'll probably see him in his armchair in the day room. No trouble at all any more; he just sits and sits and sits. Such a sweet man.'

A very short, hunched woman in a pink cardigan who had been hovering behind them suddenly tapped Alice on the arm.

'Excuse me,' she said, 'do you have any butter?'

The nurse turned around. 'No, no, Betty. This is a friend of Margery's. She doesn't have any butter for you.'

'I've got sugar and flour but I need some butter,' the woman said. 'It's on my list.' She looked at Alice plaintively. The nurse shook her head, smiling, and gave the pink-cardiganned woman a little push. 'Off you run now, Betty.'

'But –'

'I said, *Off you run now.*'

The small woman sighed and turned away, head down, mouthing, 'Sugar, flour, butter, a dozen fresh eggs. Sugar, flour, butter, a dozen fresh eggs.'

'It's not very dignified, is it, losing your mind,' said the nurse, smoothing back her hair. 'There are certain questions . . .' She stayed silent for a moment, lost inside some private reverie until Alice leaned forward and said, 'The day room?' The nurse nodded briskly and turned, and they continued down the corridor and through a second set of doors.

'And here we all are; here's the day room. There's Margery over

45

on the other side. A visitor for you, Margery! One of your old Girl Guides.'

They walked over to the neat, thin figure sitting in a straight-backed chair by the window.

'Thank you, *Sandra*,' said Mrs Austin irritably. She looked up from the crossword puzzle she'd been filling in. 'Well, well, Alice Robinson. Hello, my dear. Do have a seat.'

'Hello,' said Alice. 'You're looking well. How's your hip?'

'Insincere flattery is never becoming, Alice, but I thank you for the spirit in which the comment was directed. My hip is still doing its utmost to leave me becalmed in this place, I'm afraid, but other than that I am admirable. Perhaps you would be so kind as to pass me my teacup. It's just there on that little table. Oh dear, remember, Alice, that a Guide's fingernails are never "in mourning". You need to find a good cake of soap and a little nailbrush. How are your parents? Enjoying their trip? My youngest brother, David, he moved to Canada, you know. Wonderful fishing. And how's your young man?'

'Callum?' Alice shook her head. 'We broke up. It was a while ago.'

'Hmmm, probably for the best, if you don't mind my saying. He had very peculiar hair and I got the impression that he drank quite a bit. A person who drinks, I've always said, is no use as a Girl Guide and very little use for anything else.' Mrs Austin disapproved of Callum – especially of his receiving unemployment benefit (to support his art, he said) despite his eminent employability as a white middle-class male – but then Mrs Austin would have disapproved of a lot of the people Alice knew in London. She would have said that they had no sense of social conscience, of duty. Mrs Austin believed in duty, gratitude, fidelity, love of Great Britain and fresh air. Alice worried about: were the Girl Guides okay politically? Did the movement's imperialist and quasi-militaristic beginnings negate such perceived benefits as the

46

development of self-reliance and civic responsibility? Was civic responsibility actually desirable?

'But how are you finding it here?' said Alice, looking around at the other men and women sitting quietly in their chairs like strangers on a train. A television droned softly across the room.

'Sinister,' said Mrs Austin. 'And that nurse, Sandra, is especially sinister. Sometimes I find leaflets for funeral services slipped inside my bag. It is most disconcerting. At present I regard myself as a temporary visitor, only here until my hip heals, but the expense is beginning to concern me. I worry that I'll have to put my house on the market before I ever manage to get home to it.'

The small woman in the pink cardigan shuffled by muttering to herself.

'I wonder whether we might be able to get some biscuits to go with this tea. You sometimes can on account of visitors – the few that we have. So many of the residents here don't really make sense any more and so I suppose people think, why bother? Of course a lot of it is to do with upbringing. Do you see that man over there?'

'With the moustache? By the fireplace?'

'Very interesting chap if you catch him on a good day – stories about the navy. To my knowledge his son has been to visit him precisely twice during the last nine months. Both times to discuss the will. I believe that there's quite a large house involved. You look pale, Alice. Are you taking enough fresh air? When is this dog appearing? That will be the thing: get you outside and running about. I had a wonderful Lab once. Monarch. Which breed is yours?'

'I don't know. I don't really know that much about dogs. They've always sort of scared me.'

'You never took your Pet Care badge, did you? That was an easy one. Most girls took Pet Care. I had to rescue a small child from a mad dog once and the thing to do, if one ever attacks you, is to get a stick – or even a handkerchief if you still carry such a thing – and hold it out between your hands. Nine times out of ten the hound will go for the stick first, and that gives you a splendid chance to get in a good sharp kick. Aim for the jaw, I'd suggest. Now, could I trouble you to fetch my reading glasses? I've being trying to solve this puzzle using a magnifying glass and my arm is starting to ache rather. It's number sixteen, on the first floor.'

Alice made her way along the corridor, but quickly took what must have been a wrong turning and found herself by the kitchen. Sandra loomed up.

'I think I'm a bit lost,' Alice said. 'I'm trying to find Mrs Austin's room.'

Sandra nodded. 'It's this way. You really should have asked me in the first instance. I don't encourage people to wander just anywhere here. It upsets the residents.'

Alice made an apologetic noise.

'Follow me, please.'

They continued down the corridor and up a staircase. Alice paused on the landing and smiled. 'I've just remembered that I used to come here with the Brownies. We came carol singing.'

Sandra frowned. 'Carol singing. I may put a stop to children carol singing this year,' she said. 'It distracts the residents. I see the Lighthouse as a place of silence, of preparation and contemplation. They have no need to be reminded of youth and music and all the things that have gone away from them for ever. Not all of the other staff, I'm afraid, share my views.' She pushed open the door to Mrs Austin's small room. 'Next week we have a *juggler*.' She sighed, turned, and glimmered away from Alice, receding into the gloom of the corridor.

As a child Danny had almost drowned and since then his life had often seemed a sort of aimless freefall while he waited to find out why he'd been saved – though he understood, now that he was nineteen, that other people found this attitude off-putting. He had learned not to discuss the miraculous with strangers. He had discovered, through trial and error, that what people liked to talk about was the thing they had already talked about three or four times before; that conversations were more like train tracks than roads or footpaths. It had been suggested to Danny that he tended to fixate, that he was, perhaps, a little *intense*. He was aware that a single event need not, indeed arguably should not, be used to define and explain the whole of your existence – but it was certainly a tempting position.

'You were playing soldiers,' his mother always told him when he asked about the accident. 'You had a stick to use as a gun. It was freezing cold outside and you had green wellington boots with frog faces on the toes.'

Danny remembered running with the stick across the grass. The adults were inside the tearooms and the other children were away clambering over a fallen tree trunk. He remembered standing at the edge of the water and seeing that the ice was dirty and greyish, and not beautiful and shining as it had appeared from a distance. He remembered looking down at the smiling frogs as he stepped off from the bank on to the frozen surface.

'When the others came inside without you I went running,' said his mother. 'You'd been in the lake almost three-quarters of an hour when the men pulled you out. I thought they were giving me a corpse instead of a child. I was on my knees.'

'It's what's known as the "Mammalian Diving Reflex",' said the doctor. 'When the temperature is low enough, below twenty-one degrees centigrade, humans (especially babies and the very young) have sometimes survived for up to an hour underwater. This is a weaker version of the mechanism observed in seals and dolphins.'

'We must thank God,' said the vicar, 'for the deliverance, this weekend, of one of the youngest members of our congregation.'

When you pass through the waters I will be with you;
and through the rivers, they shall not overwhelm you;
when you walk through fire you shall not be burned,
and the flame shall not consume you.

'It's a miracle,' people said, and watched him guardedly and from a distance.

Since being asked to leave his sixth-form classes – biology, history and physics; insignificant thefts, petty rudenesses, minor infringements – Danny had worked first at the local supermarket, 'You need to develop your interpersonal skills,' they'd told him as they were letting him go, and now at the off-licence at the end of the parade, where the owner, Paul, kept him on an extended probation period and often sat mistrustfully in the back room during his shifts. Danny had never learned how to really *get on* with people. But it was unfair, he thought, that the world of gainful employment should penalize him for having been friendless as a child. The first day of school they'd marked him out as different and socially dubious: 'This is Daniel. He doesn't have a daddy so you must all be especially nice to him.'

'But university will be different,' said his mother when Danny explained that he wanted to work instead of completing his education at the local college.

How would you know? he thought but didn't say. His mother had left school at sixteen and was sensitive about the fact.

It was Monday, quiet, the graveyard day when everyone drank fruit juice or some such and the off-licence was silent except for the humming of the two upright fridges. Because it was dark outside and bright within, Danny couldn't see much through the large window at the front of the shop, only an indistinct impression of himself and the overhead lights swimming in a murky blackness. He stared instead at the glowing numbers on the digital clock by the till, willing them to flash forwards more speedily on their journey to ten thirty and the end of his shift. Sometimes, when he was left by himself, maybe sitting in his bedroom or standing like this behind the counter at the off-licence, he had the feeling that he was still alone underwater and that the world was very calm and quiet and far away. When Danny stretched his hands out he almost felt the cold green weeds brushing across his fingertips. Sometimes when he was startled out of the feeling, the trance almost, he experienced a sudden sadness, as though he'd almost reached somewhere important, a place indefinable but long sought. Other times, conversely, he woke with a sense of relief and a bitter taste in his mouth.

He ran his fingers over the front of the till. One of the CCTV cameras was always trained on the counter, which stopped him, on days he felt particularly discouraged, from slipping open the drawer and riffling through the crisp and greasy notes. With an hour still to go until closing, a brightly lipsticked woman wearing a mackintosh came in and began browsing along the shelves. Syrah, Merlot, Malbec. Chardonnay, Semillon, Sauvignon Blanc. The bottles gleamed, the most expensive wearing a faint dust shroud: the customers liked a reasonable glass of wine at the weekend but were not excessive in their tastes. Waiting for her to make a selection he watched himself on one of the monitors, brushing the lock of brown hair, the deflated quiff, down over his right eye and practising a smile, though the result, as always, was disappointingly rictal. He looked at the woman again – she had seemed familiar – and now recognized her as the neighbours' daughter. When she eventually picked a cheap red and turned towards the counter he tried to look as though he hadn't been staring. Alice lived in London and wrote long newspaper articles on art and culture and was generally intimidating. She put the bottle of wine on the counter and smiled at him, but he was too busy pretending to ignore her to notice.

No more customers came in after Alice had bought her wine. Danny was able to close up on time and then walked home, pulling his old army coat around himself against the cold. Turning into his road he could see down the hill to where the pampas grass in his front garden waved creamy flower heads above thin, bluish-green leaves, sharp like razors. There was no car in the driveway, which meant that his mother and stepfather were out, but the lights were on in the adjoining house. He was used to the neighbours, the two old people next door who had been there all his life like the beech trees at the end of the back garden and the pampas grass in front, but the daughter, faintly alarming, felt like an intrusion. She made the house seem suddenly smaller, the dividing wall between the properties thinner. He stood in the darkness of the street a moment and watched the lighted windows.

Of course it had been threaded through his childhood, the story of the house next door. A story used to keep children home, keep them close, to show them that terrible things could happen on the best, the most familiar streets. The girl had disappeared walking home from school. *Just like that. In an instant, in a moment, in a twinkling of an eye.* She had disappeared into the shadow that lurked at the bottom of the stairs, the footsteps that followed him down the alleyway, the empty house in the evening when he was too old for a babysitter (but only just) and when he barricaded himself into the front room and sat there, scared to look out of the window in case a face was looking back. He shivered and stamped his feet on the cold pavement and turned away up his own drive.

The local Anglican church was a hygienic 1930s building with no graveyard, no crypt, just a Garden of Remembrance, which seemed a grand name for the small strip of earth hedged with dark green laurels highlighted now, as Alice passed, with flaming waxy-red camellias. Next to it was the hall where the congregation gathered to drink coffee after the ten o'clock Sunday morning service. There were little glass teacups on glass saucers, and on Sundays when their parents were in charge of the kitchen – the congregation took this duty in turns – it had been Alice and Janey's job to spoon one heap of instant coffee and one heap of off-white Coffee-mate into each cup. By the sink the large metal urn gurgled ominously as the congregation queued up at the hatch and dropped their coins on to an honesty plate. They had drunk tea at home and so the taste of coffee was imbibed, always, with the idea of sociability, with a feeling of being on display.

They'd never held a service for Janey at the church. There was no body and so they believed, they had to believe, that she was out there somewhere in the world. 'A person has a right to agency, a right to disappear,' a woman from the Missing Persons Helpline had said to them once. 'A person is not obligated to stay in touch.' Alice's parents gave money to a charity that helped reunite the missing with their families, and every so often newsletters and appeals would appear in the post: stories of the presumed-deceased watching a television appeal and making contact after twenty years, of the disappeared-without-trace tracked down by caseworkers to unknown addresses in strange cities. *This is the day he'll decide to call and ask us to help him go home.*

At the small parade of shops Alice bought milk and bread, and then wandered slowly past the empty Woolworths store, the off-licence and the black-gabled Village Club (a moniker which, in this interwar suburb, always struck her as wildly aspirational). She saw her parents' neighbour coming out of the post office, pushing her fine, wispy hair back behind her ears with the usual nervous gesture as she hurried across the street. Alice's father had worked with her husband. A second marriage, was it? No. She'd been, eccentrically in their street, a single mother.

Walking on, Alice saw one or two other faces that she recognized vaguely but no one else she could name. She saw the tower blocks in their distant blue haze. The sawdust-strewn butcher's shop was gone, as was the greengrocer's, but really it was all, everywhere, utterly familiar and wherever she walked she bumped into ghosts floating around the corners, lounging at the bus stops, hanging upside down from the swings in the local recreation ground. *This is me*, she repeated to herself, *this is me walking along beside this grass verge*. She felt she was tired of experiencing the world at one remove, of interpreting other people's interpretations. She wanted, for a while, to focus on this: the damp green of the grass verge, the darker grey of the Tarmac on the road and the lighter grey of the kerb. This was the world unmediated and this was her within it. Deep in thought she looked up but didn't, at first, recognize the man getting out of the maroon car ahead of her, the morning sunshine showing up the cheapness of the fibre of his trousers, the white shirt caressing his belly just as all had longed to do when he and Alice and Janey were teenagers.

Ever since the year they'd seen a flasher by the golf course on the way to a Guide meeting (it was purple-pink, looked a little like chilled meat from the refrigerator) Janey had been obsessed by romance and the physical differences between men and women. Every Saturday they caught the bus into town with apricot lip balm smeared across their mouths and stinking of Impulse body spray

(Alice, Ocean Breeze; Janey, Siren), and Janey lounged by the driver's cab practising sex appeal while Alice sat upstairs listening to her yellow Sony Sport Walkman (waterproof). There always had to be a boy with Janey and it always had to be love; she admitted no lesser emotion.

The last time Alice had seen the man with the maroon car he'd been standing outside the local police station smoking a B&H, waiting for his mother to collect him. There had been dark shadows underneath his eyes and he'd held one arm protectively around his guitar case (the police had called him in from a band rehearsal). Alice had been walking home from town where she'd been fixing 'missing' posters to trees and noticeboards and had pretended not to see him, had been walking quickly by on the other side of the road until he called her name. She'd stopped, reluctantly, and turned back towards him, the rucksack filled with unused posters pulling down her right shoulder. He ground out the B&H with his Converse plimsoll and ran a hand through his shoulder-length, dirtily bleached hair. When she got closer she saw that the shadows under his eyes were from where the eyeliner that Janey had given him had smudged and run a little.

'They keep asking me the same questions,' Martin had said, looking horrified. 'I've told them everything I know and they just keep asking me.' He looked like a boy struggling under the cosh of a bad dream. 'When I wake up? Their voices are the first thing I hear. Their questions.' He didn't ask, *Have you heard anything?* He didn't ask, *Do you think they'll find her?* She'd always remembered that.

Now, as he locked the car and shuffled towards the estate agency on the corner, she hesitated and then called out. He looked up defensively and for a long moment Alice watched the thoughts moving behind the softened face. He ran his fingers through thinning hair. And finally 'Alice?' he said. 'Alice Robinson?'

Inside the office he made two cups of tea and they sat at opposite sides of his desk as if Alice were looking for a house to buy. Not, he said, that there had been much buying recently. Or selling. 'And I told them, I said I literally will not go that far south of the asking price. I mean, nice little semis with en-suites don't come on the market every day. This time last year they'd have been literally gagging to sign. Gagging.' Alice nodded in what she hoped was an understanding manner as Martin stared morosely at the A4 printout in front of him. Then he brightened. 'Your parents thinking of selling up? You're thinking of moving back here maybe? In need of a little flat? The Vectra's new,' he added disjointedly. 'Cruises beautifully once you get the speed up.'

Alice fingered the snow globe on his desk. Inside the glass was a little thatched cottage with a SOLD sign attached to a white picket fence. Peter would have liked the globe for his collection. She looked down at the A4 printouts of housing stock: 1960s maisonettes in a yellowish, honeycomb brick; Victorian tea-merchants' houses subdivided into flats and haunted by Scots pines; 1920s semis pretending to be detached country cottages complete with lawns and privet hedges. The longer you stared at those houses – mock-timber gables above bay windows – the stranger they seemed. An uneasy period reaching backwards for a token of stability, the security of 'the quiet old days' and the glories of the Elizabethan past.

Martin was talking again.

'Good times, good times. Playing in the band. And now . . .' he held up his hand to show the plain gold ring. 'Tara. Remember her? Your year at school, I think. Ah. You girls!'

(Everyone had wanted to be Martin's girlfriend and everyone, even the girls he treated badly, which was almost every girl, talked of him fondly and softened his behaviour with their wistful longings, like Vaseline smeared on a photographer's lens. That her sister would date him had always seemed to Alice one of life's inevitabilities.)

He leaned closer and she could smell onion on his breath. 'I can't believe it was, what, fifteen years ago we all . . . you know . . . hanging out together. Have you ever . . .?'

'No. No I haven't.' She picked up the snow globe and shook it and watched the little cottage disappear inside a storm of glitter. 'It was seventeen years.'

'Terrible business,' said Martin softly, twisting the ring on his finger. He stared past Alice, silent at last, and his anxious eyes seemed to be scanning the distance for some crowd who were late, yes, but coming even now. Some group, he believed, who were just on their way.

Sarah's Ikea-furnished kitchen smelled a little of bleach. (There had been talk of a flu pandemic on the news and Sarah worried.) She had, on the laminated worktop surface, a ceramic biscuit jar that always impressed Alice. It suggested a whole other world of organization and domesticity. Alice and Isabel's biscuits lived in crumpled packets on the coffee table. Since moving to London, she hadn't seen much of Sarah – a few birthday parties, the occasional Christmas drink – and now sitting in Sarah's kitchen the two women had run out of conversation. Alice had talked about Emily's impending visit (she was arriving that afternoon; Janey's old bed had new sheets on it) and about the baby's christening. She had admired the redecorated bathroom and heard about Matt's promotion. She wanted to smoke.

Sarah placed her ceramic biscuit jar in the middle of the table, unconsciously squeezing her always-unfamiliar waist between her hands. She'd never really got over being the fattest Girl Guide in the troop, the twelve-year-old whose breasts and stomach strained the buttons of her blue uniform. The beefy kid who caused the rope bridge to sag dangerously when her patrol took their turn at the assault course. Alice would already be over the other side, jigging up and down encouragingly while Janey slouched against a tree complaining that it was all stupid; secretly desperate to win.

'So where's Matt?' said Alice.

'Oh, just in the office I suppose. At work. Where else would he be?'

Ah yes, work, that thing that people did; that place where she should have been instead of drinking tea and looking at babies.

'He's always late home just now though, worrying that all these problems with the economy are going to end up affecting voting at the local elections. We're worried about what that will mean for him job-wise . . .'

'Are you planning on going back to teaching then?'

'I don't know. Not yet, not while –' Sarah indicated the sleeping baby with her head and extracted a custard cream from the biscuit jar. 'I never understand why people have children if they're not prepared to look after them properly. Doesn't it seem selfish? Anyway, so how is, um, Callum?'

'We broke up. It was a mutual thing.'

'Oh.' Sarah looked embarrassed. 'And how are those friends I met at your thirtieth? You know, the boy and girl.'

'Peter and Isabel?'

'Yes, that's it. Peter and Isabel; they were so sweet. Not like everybody else there. I don't want to sound rude but, well, Matt and I thought there was just something a bit *superior* about the attitudes of most of those people. I had this idea they were looking down on me all evening as if I couldn't *possibly* have anything interesting to say. Matt thought the same.'

'No, no, of course not; I think it's just the way their haircuts come across in a conversation. Anyway, they sort of have to be like that. It stops them getting depressed because they're all tired of being aspiring creative whatevers. Superficial superiority is the only thing they have.'

Sarah looked unconvinced. The baby woke up and she bounced him on her lap. He was beautiful with a rather solemn baby-face and dressed, for some reason, in an outfit that made him look like a miniature bear.

'That's a nice Babygro,' said Alice. 'He looks very . . . ursine.'

'Thanks.' The baby started drooling. 'It was a christening present. Ooh, do you want to see our holiday pics from France? Will you hold him for a sec?'

Alice cradled the bear-baby awkwardly, smelling his sweet doughy scent. Next to the biscuit jar on the table was Sarah's 'baby life check' chart. There, in blue type, was a list of all the things the baby should be doing at two months, three, six, a year. Wouldn't it be nice, Alice thought, if the charts could carry on? A chart that told you precisely what stage you should have reached by eighteen years, twenty, thirty-four. 'I wish I could speak French,' she said. 'It always feels so shameful not to be able to speak another language because, you know, everyone understands English.'

They looked at the holiday photographs.

'We took the car and drove through the Channel Tunnel. I was terrified. I kept imagining it leaking, the feeling of being underneath all those tonnes of water.'

The bear-baby started to grizzle and Alice bounced him tentatively. 'What time is it?'

'Five?'

'Oh bugger. Oh. Sorry.' She flapped her hand as if to waft the word from the bear-baby's ears. 'I have to go and meet Emily.'

Sarah nodded. 'I need to start cooking.' She reached out for the bear-baby.

Alice stood up. 'I forgot to say, I bumped into Martin yesterday.'

Sarah raised her eyebrows.

'He seems different.'

'How do you mean? I know he's put on weight,' Sarah felt her waist, 'and he's losing his hair. Do you remember how it used to be bleached like, like that singer? From Nirvana.'

'I don't think that's what I meant.'

'Mmmm. Well. I haven't really spoken to him recently. I never thought we had much in common. I think Matt sees him at the pub occasionally. *Very* occasionally. He married that girl whose mother had the German shepherd. Tara. Anyway, I'm surprised that *you* would want to see him. What could you possibly have to say to someone like that?'

Alice nodded. 'Yes, you're right. What could I have to say? There's nothing really, is there? Well, goodbye.'

'Good luck with the little cousin. Bring her over sometime. I'll make cake.'

Alice walked to the station, stepped off the pavement once to avoid a group of schoolchildren rushing past in the opposite direction, their loud conversation filled with unintelligible words. She was feeling as, she remembered, she always did now after seeing Sarah: that she had been gently disapproved of, that despite being the elder she had been pushed firmly into some junior role. She felt as though she had aimed for sophistication and ended up a dubious debauchee. 'You used to look up to me when we were teenagers,' she'd said jokingly, and saw a look of polite alarm spread across Sarah's face.

At the train station she bought a cup of coffee from the concession on the forecourt, stood drinking it and watching a stream of commuters lurch one after the other up the slope from the platform. With their faces illuminated by the harsh station lighting each one paused a moment at the ticket barrier, on display to the forecourt like a star at a premiere, like, Alice thought, an anonymous figure captured by a street photographer and made briefly significant.

When she finally appeared Emily was easy to recognize: a small figure marching along the platform wearing a tight silver jacket with a voluminous fur-lined hood and pulling a large suitcase. She was tanned and glowing in the middle of the pale wintry crowd. Alice waved from behind the ticket barrier.

'I'm Alice,' she said, reaching out her hand. Emily looked curious but extended her own fingers and the two of them shook. Then Alice realized that she should, of course, have hugged the girl, embraced her, and she laughed to cover her embarrassment. Emily rolled her eyes. They got into a taxi because of the suitcase.

'How was the flight? Did you sleep?'

Emily shrugged. 'It was okay.'

'And your mum? She's well?'

'Uh huh.'

Outside a fine drizzle had begun. One of the windows was open a crack and the smell of rain mixed with exhaust fumes came through, making Alice feel queasy.

'I expect you're tired so we'll just go back to the house now, unpack, and this evening we'll maybe get a takeaway? You'll have to tell me if there's anything you particularly want to do while you're here. You know, in town. Buckingham Palace, Tower of London . . . Emily?'

She looked over and saw that her cousin had plugged in a pair of headphones and was nodding slightly to the beat. Alice leaned back. Outside the dampened suburbs moved by, and between the train station and the house there was a frontier sense, still, of the streets having been carved from woods and fields instead of grown, organically, from a church, a row of workers' cottages, a Roman settlement. History was shallow here and just two generations back all the local families had been living somewhere else. The taxi passed the playing fields of the local public school and then the red-brick primary where Alice and Janey had learned to spell and multiply and subtract. Tinny music leaked out of Emily's headphones and her eyes were closed.

They pulled up outside the house and the driver lifted Emily's suitcase out of the boot. Alice pulled it up the drive with her cousin trailing after. Inside she turned up the thermostat to make the house warmer, more welcoming, while Emily sat silently at the table, her thin shoulders hunched under her jacket, the hood pulled up and the pale fur haloing around her face, still dressed for the outdoors as if the whole horrible mess might end at any moment and someone would tell her to go home.

'Would you like some tea? A glass of water?'

'Water? I need to take my supplements.'

Alice filled a glass at the tap and passed it to her.

'Um, do you have any bottled water? I heard that every glass of tap water you drink in London has already been drunk, like, seven times before. Which is totally gross.'

'I've got some orange juice?'

Emily nodded. 'I'm tired,' she said. 'Can I go lie down?'

The houses in England are so small, Emily thought. So cramped up all together. On the train she'd tried not to imagine how many times each mouthful of air had been breathed, tried not to think of all the yellow-toothed, gummy, halitosis mouths it had passed through. The English were famous for their bad dental work.

In the bedroom of her aunt and uncle's house she opened the door of the wardrobe meaning to unpack, but the space was already filled with clothes. She pulled out a few – a short suede skirt, a grungy grey jumper with holes in the sleeves, a hideous tie-dye vest top – her missing cousin's cast-offs presumably. No one could even be bothered to empty a wardrobe for her. The whole room, now she looked at it properly, was dusty and seriously needed to be cleaned. The walls were thick with old posters as if nothing had ever been taken down, and so some long-haired boy standing in a field with daisies was covered by the one who killed himself was covered by a group of thin, pale men wearing suits. Underneath the bed were a pair of purple sneakers and a pair of high, faux crocodile-skin platform shoes. It was sort of creepy.

She lay down. Alice was outside smoking and because the window was slightly ajar the smell of burning tobacco had come into the room. In Emily's opinion only poor, uneducated people smoked. Alice, she thought, was generally sort of unhealthy-looking – though not in a fat way. It was hard to describe, or maybe it was just her age. Emily ran her fingers over her forehead and felt the faintest beginnings of a set of lines. She couldn't begin to imagine the daily-faced horror of being as old as Alice. On a corkboard above the bed was tacked a curling, yellowed school timetable and a calendar turned to an August in that great unreality of time before Emily was born. She sat up and pushed the window closed, shivered and wrapped the duvet around her. So this was what jetlag felt like. She rubbed oil-free moisturizer into her face and dabbed anti-ageing gel on to the delicate skin beneath her eyes. Everything was so dry from the aeroplane. To prevent her hair from breaking while she slept, she wrapped her pillow in the blue silk scarf borrowed secretly from her mother before the trip. She smoothed hand cream up and down each finger and put on the thin cotton gloves that she always wore to bed. They made the hand cream work harder. Also, she had long nails and was strangely distrustful of her sleeping self, afraid that unconscious and dreaming she might claw her own face. The small alarm clock on the bedside table showed seven-oh-five, but it felt already as though she had been awake all night.

Determinedly Emily began working her way through chapter six of *Choose to be Happy: How to Take Back Control*, but her mind was spidering. The whole thing had happened so quickly, which was typical of her mother, a woman who considered herself spontaneous and fun-loving. Carol had never planned Emily's childhood treats in advance, instead deciding suddenly, on a whim, that they must at once have a trip to the fair, the lake, the movies. As well as depriving her daughter of the exquisite agonies of childhood anticipation, this had the effect of leaving her with the heightened sense that life was something unpredictable that rushed at you and that you had to be, always, a little on guard against.

Choose to be Happy wavered in Emily's hands. Each time her eyelids closed it became more and more difficult to force them open again. England. This would be educational, her mother said. Emily was unconvinced. Educational would have been learning a foreign language. Or driving lessons. This interlude was, frankly, a distraction from Emily's goal, which was to grow herself up as quickly as

66

possible, get to college, meet her future husband and begin what she already viewed as her real life. She had a timetable worked out that required her to be engaged by twenty-two, married by twenty-three. Presumably kids after that. By Alice's age she planned to be driving a Grand Cherokee. England could not be considered a part of real life.

'You don't mind, do you?' Carol had said. 'It's just that I want a proper honeymoon this time. That's what went wrong with Paul. We never got things off on the right footing. I'm going to miss you, sweetie.' (Her father, Paul, and now Larry. Emily thought that her mother was always marrying the man who fitted with the person she wanted to be and not the person she was, and so her relationships were always out of sync.) Also, she and her mother had not been getting along so well recently – which was a polite way of saying that she often looked at Carol and was consumed with intense feelings of hatred and irritation that caused her to wish, sometimes vocally, that she had never been born. She found her mother wanting in several key areas. The therapist had blamed it on the divorce, but mainly her father leaving hadn't bothered Emily as much as people told her it had, or would. Mainly she preferred life at home without the sarcasm at breakfast, the shouting at lunchtime, the heavy silences during the evening meal.

At least in England she wouldn't have to hang out with Larry, who had a wheedling voice and uncomfortable eyes. (Her mother's taste in men was definitely suspect and, she thought, getting worse.) She'd heard that Larry had once been arrested for drunk-driving – he'd been so many times over the limit that even the arresting officer had been scandalized and repeated the story, through a buddy, to a large portion of the town – but when she'd casually let that one slip out over dinner (this was before the marriage) Carol had just smiled dreamily and said, 'Is that so?' as if she'd been told that her fiancé had once won a fishing competition or that in his early twenties he had spent a year helping orphans in Africa. Emily frowned and then immediately made herself relax her facial muscles. Few situations in life were worth permanent facial scarring. She recognized that much at least. She sniffed and turned over and then quite suddenly fell asleep, dreaming that she was back in California, standing in the road outside of her old kindergarten and trying unsuccessfully to hitch a ride. The cars sped past without stopping and then she looked down and realized with shame that she was wearing her cousin's gruesome purple sneakers and in the dream she started to cry with frustration because everyone had seen her and because she knew, she was convinced, that she had put on quite another pair of shoes earlier that morning.

Emily complained of the cold; it got into her bones. And there was very little between Emily's bones and the English weather. Alice, worrying about heating costs and global warming, found an old cable-knit jumper for Emily to wear, but whenever she went out her cousin turned up the thermostat and Alice would return to find the jumper discarded on the sofa in the living room. Instead, Emily would be lounging at the computer in her minimal vest and knickers or sitting on the sofa flipping through one of her glossy women's magazines.

In the house Emily kept mostly to herself, but Alice sometimes had the curious sensation that the girl was constantly ahead of her, of Emily having always left a room moments before Alice entered it. In the bathroom she found long, blonde hairs stuck damply to the shower wall. In the kitchen there was a trail of crumbs around the breadbin and a knife shivering on the edge of the counter. In the living room she almost tripped over a half-drunk cup of camomile tea surrounded by pink-stained discarded balls of cotton wool. In the dining room the curtains rustled as if someone had just run by. Emily had taken it upon herself to tidy away all of Janey's belongings (Alice hadn't told her mother yet) and the bedroom was now as neat and hygienic as a hospital ward, but she left bits of herself all over the rest of the house like an animal marking its territory. Alice was sure that things had been moving in her own room – a book not where she left it, a lipstick or a five-pound note apparently missing, a bottle of scent seeming to have travelled from the front to the back of her dressing table.

Now Alice could hear, faintly, the sound of the television: Emily had been lying for hours on the sofa in the living room, staring at the screen. She picked up some films from a pile by her bed and went downstairs.

'Hey' – throwing the plastic cases on to the coffee table – 'want to watch a movie? I bought a whole bunch back from London.'

Emily shrugged but leaned over and began looking through the selection. 'I don't know any of these,' she said eventually. 'Isn't there anything in English?'

They watched Tarkovsky's *The Sacrifice* and Alice poured herself a glass of wine. Maybe this would become a regular thing that they did together. When she was Emily's age she would have loved to have had someone show her these films. On screen the man walked away from his burning house and Emily, watching, twisted a strand of hair around her finger as the camera pulled away to show the fire reflected in the pools of water. When the credits came up, Alice turned expectantly to her cousin. Emily shrugged. 'I guess I'd rather have seen something in English,' she said, and yawned. 'Can I watch TV now?'

'Right, okay, sorry,' said Alice, thinking, *I probably shouldn't have started with Tarkovsky.*

Emily got up and flicked through the channels until she found a quiz show. Alice leaned back and noticed a wisp of spider's web hanging from the flower-shaped light fitting in the centre of the room, but she could see, from where she was slumped on the sofa, that it was too high for her to reach to pull it down and so she stayed where she was, staring vacantly at Emily's quiz show and working her way through the rest of the bottle of wine.

'Tom and Pam's niece,' said his mother, tucking and then re-tucking her thin hair back behind her ears. 'She's about your age, maybe a bit younger. I think there's something wrong with the washing machine.' She held up a damp shirt. Turned it this way and this way in the light. 'It's not draining properly on a thirty cycle, but it's what you're supposed to use. For the environment. She's . . . something . . . Emma?'

Emily, said Danny silently, feeling the secret weight of the name. Earlier that morning he had watched her exercising in the back garden, standing in the middle of the lawn stretching upwards, fingertips pointing towards the white sky, and then down, bending at the waist until her palms were flat against the grass. When she'd bent over he'd seen, and it was like a private signal, a flash of bright pink thong.

'Um. I've got to get ready for work,' he said, standing up. 'I'll be late for my shift.'

'Is that the time?' His mother glanced at the kitchen clock. 'Now I'll have to drive to the baths.' She turned away, looking for her keys. 'You should come swimming next time you've a day off; you never use my pass any more. And bring some friends. We've had a new slide put in – though maybe you're too old for that now.' She looked at him worriedly.

'Yeah,' said Danny. 'Yes. I should stop by.' He flashed his rictus grin at her, colluding briefly in the delusion that he had not just *a* friend but a *multiple* of friends. A group of guys who liked to hang out on a Saturday afternoon dive-bombing and eating Mars bars from the snack machine. In reality the last time he'd been to the leisure centre where his mother worked as a receptionist he'd gone through all the lockers looking for unguarded change and had swapped his old trainers for a pair of newish Nikes. He probably just wasn't what the careers adviser called a 'people person'. Conversation, for example. With him it was always famine or feast; either he couldn't think of anything to say or else the words came out too quickly and for too long, tumbling and nonsensical as eager but oversized puppies trying to hump an unwary leg. People backed away.

Upstairs he ran a bath, sprinkling into the avocado tub a handful of bath salts and watching the water turn strongly pink like photographs he'd seen of the sea around the Faroe Islands during whaling season. He undressed, leaving on only the gold St Christopher, the sometime dog-headed patron saint of travellers that his mother insisted he wear. Naked, down in the steaming tub, his skin looked white near the surface but shaded away steadily into pink. With his ears underwater, only a flat moon of face breaking the pink surface and his hair floating around him like seaweed, everything was muffled. The echoey popping noises of his inner ear canal. Taking a breath, Danny sank beneath the water, down into the pinkness, breathing out a stream of silver bubbles. Thinking, *What would it be like to really drown this time?* He held his breath, counting, feeling all his features thicken and swell before exploding upwards once more into the air.

He lay back. Danny's body was, frankly, a disappointment to him. It lacked grandeur and muscular definition. Across his narrow chest the skin took on a bluish tint and his ribs were shadows on a snowfield. *You look like a ghost.* Alive, yet something clung to him: a shadow on the lung, a murmur in the heart. He believed that in coming back from the dead he should have gained some knowledge, some wisdom, some enlightenment, but instead he just felt set apart. He thought of the familiar Bible stories; he was like Lazarus, Jairus's daughter, the son of the widow of Nain. Would they have been thankful for their second chances or would the idea of a further sixty, seventy years seem suddenly trivial after that glimpse of unending time?

Downstairs the front door opened and then closed. The sound of the car engine being switched on, idling, and then pulling away. The house was quiet and still again, and Danny lay there wallowing until the bath water began to cool. He thought of Emily sitting next door and smiled as he began soaping up his hair.

In the kitchen Alice found herself pushing aside piles of unwashed plates to make a space at the table. She'd spent the morning finishing a first-year student's essay on the poetry of William Blake (requested standard: 2:1), and today she was supposed to be writing about the British Empire. In front of her was a map from 1912 showing all the pink patches on the globe. Most of the British Empire, when you looked at it like that, was composed of Upper Canada. She lit a rollie and smoked for a while.

Emily sidled in, switched the kettle on and glanced meaningfully at the ashtray. She opened the window to let a blast of cold air sweep the room, leaned back against the kitchen counter, arms folded over the words *gold digga* written across the front of her vest top.

Alice shivered. 'You might as well write "prostitute" and be done with it,' she muttered as the boiling kettle gathered itself for a final hectic rush of steam.

Emily stared at her blankly. 'One of my friends sent me a link the other day.'

'Yes?' said Alice, wondering whether she should write something about the Boston Tea Party.

'So you really threw up on live radio? Brutal! Didn't you just, like, want to *die*?'

'Yes,' said Alice. 'Yes, thank you.'

Shaking her head, Emily poured boiling water on to a Detox tea bag. Alice didn't think Emily had anything to detox from; her cousin was the most health-conscious person she'd ever met. Emily didn't even drink caffeine. She followed diet plans and imbibed preventative medication with the strict devotion of a novitiate in a particularly unforgiving order. Emily smirked at Alice, flicked her silky hair and wandered back to the living room. Alice got up and closed the window with too much force.

'Let's go to town,' she called out. 'I'll show you the local sights.'

Ooh, said Janey sarcastically. *The sights!*

And you're not really helping here, you know, said Alice, going to look for her coat. *You need to work on that whole positive-attitude thing.*

They rode the bus past the blocks of offices by the roundabout, and then wandered through the huge, covered shopping centre, which was all ferns, fountains and beige faux-marble. Past a strip of bars advertising happy hours and smart-casual dress codes, they stopped outside the local college and watched a group of teenagers skating desultorily on the concrete forecourt. 'But why don't you have a car?' was all that Emily said. Alice sighed. After she'd moved to London the suburbs had tended to dwindle into caricature, into a two-dimensional setting for the stories of provincial life she sometimes experimented with at dinner parties. Now that she was back among the familiar streets she kept noticing things, such as the way that in the shopping centre everything had become a little shinier, a little more charming and remote. Only the post office, Alice thought, remained immured in a sort of 1980s brownness. It looked shabby and inefficient, the sort of place where human error could still occur.

In a café in one of the department stores they ordered coffees. Alice spooned the froth from the top of her cappuccino. (Her mother always used to order that when they were out, was always careful to refuse a sprinkling of 'fattening' chocolate powder. Alice remembered sitting opposite her, playing with the large, roughly cut nuggets of brown sugar that looked like pieces of amber.) Emily's blonde hair fell down over her face as she started texting someone. Alice tried to think of something to say: the trip was beginning to feel as awkward as a teenage first date.

There was a young man sitting across from them on one of the tall bar-stools. Alice reached over and touched Emily's arm, 'Check out that guy? He's sort of cute, no? Hey, maybe he thinks we're sisters!' Emily looked visibly disturbed by the suggestion. That morning, coming downstairs, Alice had felt her cousin's disapproving gaze sweep over her outfit: high-waisted black trousers that tapered at the ankles, a cream shirt, pearls and a black beret. Sturdy brown lace-up shoes and a silk scarf. Perhaps the slash of red lipstick (still Chanel, New York Red) was too much? She caught her reflection in the mirror behind the counter and suddenly couldn't decide if she looked artistic and bohemian (that had been the idea) or more like a crazy bag lady.

Emily pouted. 'How much longer do we have to stay out?'

Alice froze, her coffee cup part-way to her mouth. This was supposed to be fun. A treat. Emily could at least have *pretended*. She put down her cup and tried not to sound offended or defiant. 'When I've finished this we'll go back,' she said. 'Why don't you go and look at the shop windows or something?'

Emily shrugged and slipped up from her chair, threw her silver jacket over her shoulder and sauntered off. Alice watched her go. She tried to enjoy what was left of her coffee, smiled at the man by the counter until, catching her reflection once more, she realized that she had a faint chocolate-coffee moustache above her lip. Emily, who had moved silently back inside, came up behind her and whispered in her ear, 'No offence, cousin, but don't you think he's a little *young* for you?'

Alice had trouble sleeping. At night she populated her racetrack with fluffy white sheep for counting and then she imagined herself standing at the top of the grey stand aiming a gun at them, exploding them into red rosettes one after one after one. It was disturbingly satisfying.

Communications with the outside world were sporadic. After she'd turned down several offers to 'do a really big, serious piece for us now that you're not tied up with *Meta*', the magazines and newspapers she usually wrote for had stopped calling: her work was popular, yes, but there were plenty of other arts journalists in London and the editors would only be rebuffed so many times before moving down their lists of contacts. Also some of them found her new lack of enthusiasm unflattering, choosing to interpret it as an unspoken criticism of their life choices. In the last week she'd received only two texts: one from Isabel to say that the dog delivery was delayed, and one from a man she'd been for drinks with a couple of times before the New York trip. (He used to shout at advertising hoardings; she hadn't seen a future in it.)

On the television she got depressed watching the news: starving children, mutilated children, disappearing children. Then she felt guilty because she was co-opting the children into her general malaise – that concern for the starving children was a symptom of her despair instead of a cause. The starving children deserved to be a cause at least.

Sometimes she visited Mrs Austin at the Lighthouse. 'Do your duty,' said Mrs Austin. 'Help your fellow creature and don't mind if other people are funking.' In Mrs Austin's world there was a code, and if you followed that code there was a fine chance that everything would work out for the best. *Think what is the right thing to do and do it at once.* The code never suspected that a person might have difficulties with that basic premise. That a person might not know exactly *what is the right thing to do.* For instance, is it okay to demand political change, ethical governmental policy, the enforcement of human rights, before sending foreign aid? Is it possible to distinguish between the deserving and the undeserving poor? How much attention does a child really need? How nice must the housing be? The neighbourhood? How much money should be spent when attempting to keep alive a three-month premature baby? What about liver transplants for alcoholics?

Days slipped through her fingers with nothing to show at the end of them except an uncomfortable itch always somewhere slightly out of reach, somewhere that couldn't quite be scratched. She felt diffuse and either that nothing had any meaning or that everything had too much. She watched a raven bobbing on the lawn. Ravens are the only birds who play, she remembered reading that somewhere, the only birds with leisure time. One particularly bad day her greatest achievement was to gather up the post accumulating on the doormat. There had been a stage, when she was still living at home, of hiding Janey's letters. Those few envelopes expectantly addressed and mailed. Those one or two most random spheres where Janey's disappearance still hadn't occurred, where she still existed. (A local photographic service, a magazine's subscription bureau, a nightclub offering eighteenth-birthday parties.) She'd hidden the letters because somehow every time her parents contacted another service, another institution, Janey went away a little more completely.

Through the kitchen windows a pot of early flowering geraniums that should have been brought inside for the winter flared up pink against the black. Alice flicked the light switch to reveal a mass of dirty plates piled on the work surface, some coated with the congealed remains of meals. The sink was clogged with used tea bags. The lid of the bin was balanced a clear five centimetres above the rim on a pile of just-fragrant rubbish. The tops of the microwave, the fridge, the cooker, were dusty. She went into the living room where Emily was lying on her back on the carpet staring blankly at the TV, bending and stretching her legs. An advert for Sofa World was playing: *Mums happy because of the choice; Dad's happy because of the price.*

'You know, Emily,' Alice said, 'you could always do some cleaning or something to help out. The dishes in the sink for instance?'

'Why?'

'Er . . . because you live here? And because it's filthy?'

Conversations with Emily always seemed to involve more question marks than they did with other people. Now she responded by bursting into tears and rushing from the room with 'You're not my mother!' hurled backwards down the stairs.

'Thank God,' said Alice to the bookcases in the empty room. (*Fifty English Houses to Visit.* Books on gardening. A Catherine Cookson novel. Several unread volumes of faux-leather hardbacks with gold emboss: the poetry of Tennyson and Kipling, Defoe's *Robinson Crusoe.* Her parents described themselves as 'not big readers'.)

She sighed and went back into the kitchen; she had always been a terrible housekeeper. Now she should scrape the food off the plates by the sink. But that would mean emptying the bin and there were no more bin bags. She dabbed half-heartedly at the crumbs by the toaster before giving up. Her mother would be suitably horrified. She had once described Alice's kitchen in London as 'sluttish', though Alice was fairly certain that her mother didn't understand the secondary meaning of the word.

The front door opened and banged shut. Emily walking out. She should call after her, find out where she was going, but she couldn't summon the energy. And then there was the guilty pleasure of being alone in the house; the whole building seemed to breathe and relax with the reverberations of the slammed door. She sat down to begin a second-year essay on Wordsworth's *The Prelude* for a Tuesday deadline. Romanticism, Alice thought, could be defined by an absence of humour. A poem by Wordsworth or Tennyson, or a painting by one of the Pre-Raphaelites, relied on the straight face; the work was too easily parodied to withstand a humorous glance. And perhaps it is in this absence of humour, she continued in her imaginary essay, that romanticism most differs from classicism or from the modern and postmodern – which are, of course, essentially other forms of classicism. Emily, like Janey, seemed to lack the ability to laugh at herself. *You're not my mother!* Jesus.

Two hours later, when Emily still hadn't returned, Alice began to repent. Emily huddled by a bus shelter accosted by drunken men; Emily walking down a dark alleyway and hearing footsteps behind her; Emily in a police station saying, 'No, I live with my cousin. Of course she lets me walk the streets alone at night.' Rohypnol in half a pint of Foster's. Emily's mobile rang and rang out.

Clock-watching, she found that her guilt was edged with anger. If Emily had wanted to go out then she, Alice, would have been sympathetic if only Emily had said something instead of disappearing. Maybe they could have gone somewhere together. One evening when Alice was fourteen and bored she'd sneaked away and caught the train to London. At Victoria she'd bought French fries from McDonald's and stood in front of the clacking timetables watching the crowds of people and not knowing where to go. A man lurched past her, grabbed her briefly by the arm and hissed, 'You're usin'' before disappearing out of the station. London, with all its excitements, was so close, and she stood there eating her cooling chips and waiting for something to happen, some adventure. Then she had turned around and caught the next train home.

Nervously, Alice drifted upstairs to Janey's bedroom – Emily's bedroom now. She marvelled at the crisp duvet cover, the hairbrush and moisturizer and anti-wrinkle cream (at sixteen!) neatly arrayed on top of the chest of drawers in front of the smear-free, dust-free mirror. Janey, her books and records, was gone. To the right of the hairbrush a cathedral of pills and vitamins in pots, tubes, blister-packs. A plastic canister with STAY HEALTHY LONGER printed around it, the promise of inevitable demise locked into the cheery red font. On the windowsill was the copy of *Choose to be Happy*, marked and referenced with fluorescent yellow Post-it notes.

Relax, said Janey. *Have a drink*. Alice nodded and went downstairs and poured herself a glass of Merlot. She wondered whether she should call someone. She wanted to share the burden of know-ledge. She wanted to be able to say to the police, *At ten thirty I called X and they said not to worry; they said she'd come home soon*. She wanted it to be *not her fault*. She could call Carol in the States. But then prob-ably Emily would soon be back. Certainly she would be back at any moment. (Suddenly the bottle of wine was almost empty.) Alice opened the front door and stood watching for the small figure that wasn't there. She smelled, underneath the late frost which sparkled on the Tarmac, the clear green fragrance of vegetation in the night air. She rolled a cigarette and smoked it, leaning against the plastic frame of the porch, seeing a light come on and go off on the other, mirror-image porch of the neighbours' house. Around her the quiet mysteries of suburbia were in the perfumed thickness of the silently lighted houses, the thickness of so many private lives together and separated. The mysteries were in the almost-countryside. They were in the dark alleyways, quiet railway bridges, empty cul-de-sacs, chained, railed parks at night-time.

Alice shivered and went back inside. In the drinks cabinet, opened approximately twice a year, once on Christmas Day and once on New Year's Eve, there was an ancient bottle of sherry, a Scottish whisky, an eternal bottle of Angostura bitters. She poured the whisky. She walked to the mantelpiece and stood resting her chin on the varnished wood, on the layer of dust, her eyes level with the top of a china bell ornament. She nudged it with her nose and it tinkled in the quiet, high and thin and lacking any tunefulness. She drank the whisky. The clock on the mantelpiece – her grandmother's old clock, ugly but now elevated to the status of heirloom – ticked loudly towards twelve in her left ear and her vision was starting to blur in interesting ways. Everything was out of focus excepting the china bell, which remained startlingly lucid with its decoration of purple and yellow pansies. Outside a dog barked sharply.

The photograph of Janey smiled at her from above the television. (Always smiling, always convinced that everyone loved her.) How quickly her sister had taken on that slight sheen of unreality usually reserved for the dead. When Alice was younger she had suspected that her parents suspected she knew the answer. Would have liked to have been able to slice open her head and sift through the grey matter inside. And for a long time Alice failed to contradict this impression because she was hurt that her sister had, in fact, said nothing. Alice hadn't wanted to admit how little, in the end, Janey had relied on her. Even now, though, and especially in the early hours of the morning, she'd find herself wondering whether there was something she should have seen, could have done. There was always just enough hope, Alice thought, to keep you hanging on in there. Just enough hope, she thought, could send a person crazy. A psychic had told them that Janey was living with a man in a cold, mountainous country; another that her body was buried less than a mile from their house. For a long time there were unconfirmed sightings: a blonde girl answering Janey's description was seen on a cross-Channel ferry, at an airport, in a shopping centre in Gateshead, working behind a bar on a Greek island. Then there were the anniversary pieces published in local newspapers with strange, frightening computer-aged photographs that had been slowly, year by year, turning Janey's face into something unrecognizable. Her skin in the computer images was the pink of a stick of seaside rock and appeared to be coated in shiny plastic.

Somebody had once pointed out to Alice that if the sun disappeared it would take eight and a half minutes (the speed of light) for us to notice that anything had gone wrong. For eight and a half doomed minutes we'd see it still, lingering like a ghost in the sky, and not know that we, also, were already ghosts, already dead. Alice often thought of the last day of Janey like that – that there must have been a moment, a moment before the confirmed moment, when it was already too late, though nobody had understood a thing. At night, of course, the transition to total darkness would take a little longer: the planets, the little islands ranged through space, would wink out one by one as they took it in turn to reflect the very last of the sun's light. It would be like watching an apartment block at the end of a day, the inhabitants one after another switching off the lights in their respective windows.

She had a sort of atavistic urge to bring her hands together in prayer. *Please, please, please let her be.* It happened like that sometimes, caught her off-guard. A hymn, heard by chance on the radio, still suggested a sort of solemn, comforting happiness, like walking through a tree-lined field on a fine autumn day. She should phone. Who? She should go out looking for her. But wait. Don't make it real yet. You should understand this, she was thinking. Enjoy the moment of not-knowing. The innocent moment. Reach out one finger now and push the bell gently towards the edge of the mantelpiece until a quarter of it is trembling over empty space.

Janey watched her from across the room. *She'll be fine,* said Janey, *don't be so dramatic.* She hacked a cough as if she'd been smoking too much. She stretched out a hand towards Alice and the bell tipped gently over the edge, smashed on the tiles with a little porcelain explosion and, as if summoned by the sound, the front door opened. *See,* said Janey.

Alice put down the whisky glass feeling suddenly clear-headed as anger fought with relief. 'Emily,' she called from the fireplace. 'We need to talk.'

Her cousin came in wearing the silver jacket and slumped down in a chair with her hands clasped between her bony knees, staring at the carpet. Alice stood with her back to the mantelpiece like a stern Victorian paterfamilias. 'Well?' she said finally. 'Where were you? Why was your phone switched off?'

Emily shrugged. 'Sorry?'

Alice picked up the whisky glass. It was empty. 'It's one in the morning. I can't believe you'd be so thoughtless.'

Emily widened her eyes, looking hurt. 'I'm not. I had to make a phone call. A private phone call. And I wanted to walk. I was *safe*. I'm sixteen. I don't need babysitting.'

Alice looked at the clock again. It was five in the afternoon in California. It was probably sunny. 'I don't care. I'm phoning your mother. I'm not taking responsibility for you if you're going to behave like this.'

Emily shrugged again and went to get up.

'No, stay here, you can explain yourself to her first.'

Alice handed over the phone and went to sit in the dirty kitchen. She heard Emily muttering into the receiver. Peter and Isabel were bringing the dog next week. She should try to clean. She missed Peter – a thought she immediately squashed downwards. She missed Peter *and* Isabel.

'What's all this then, Emily?' said Larry, who'd come inside from the barbecue to answer the telephone. 'Not improving, eh? Up to the old tricks, eh?'

'I want to speak to Mom,' said Emily, ignoring him.

'Oh sweetie, I'm just so disappointed,' said Carol. Her voice was filled with gin and tonic in the way that Emily hated. 'You were always such a kind, polite little girl. I don't know what's happened to you. Daddy's disappointed too.'

'You've already phoned Daddy? In Florida?'

'Of course not; I mean your new daddy. Anyway, sweetie, think of poor Alice. It must have brought back all those terrible, terrible memories. Remember that your cousin, your *other* cousin, was just your age when she disappeared. What was Alice supposed to think with you running off? That it was happening all over again? The waiting, that's the thing, the helplessness . . .' A gin-tinged sob rushed down the telephone wires. 'You're never the same after a thing like that. It just *haunts* you.'

Emily handed the phone to Alice and walked slowly back upstairs. When she was out the thought hadn't crossed her mind, but now she couldn't help wondering: what would have happened if she'd kept on walking away from the house? But anyway, why would a person even want to do something like that? Emily imagined a dark figure looming up behind her and shivered. In her bedroom (Janey's bedroom) she stood in front of the mirror and slowly took off her silver jacket to reveal a powder-blue T-shirt with *hypermodern* written across the chest. She felt a little cold. She was a good person. The world doesn't revolve around you, Emily. She smoothed back her hair and rubbed her hands across her face from the centre outwards, flattening the skin back like a facelift until she looked like someone strange and other. Then she walked back downstairs to find Alice.

They pulled on pink rubber gloves, swept up the rubbish and ran the hot tap and put dishes into the sink to soak. Emily hummed to herself as she shuffled around with the broom making little piles of dirt. She couldn't believe that her aunt and uncle didn't have a dishwasher. It was so *primitive*. At home, Maria from Mops and Buckets came over once a week to clean. Maria, who usually looked stern and downcast, made Emily uncomfortable. But occasionally – very occasionally – she would sing songs in Spanish. Emily rinsed the first load of dishes and stacked them on the draining board and emptied the sink before filling it up again, marvelling, as ever, at the impracticality of the two-tap system. Alice kept stopping to roll cigarettes, which she smoked standing at the back door, but despite this they made good progress. Emily found a cloth and steeled herself to open the refrigerator. Holding her breath, she started pulling out boxes and cartons of inedible food and, because there were no bin liners, threw them into plastic grocery bags. The greatest horror was the vegetable drawer, which had turned into a stinking sea of grey goo, but she rose confidently even to that challenge. She thought her therapist would be pleased to see her being so constructive – though it was sometimes hard to tell, with therapists.

Emily thought about Janey while she worked. 'I don't get it,' she said finally. 'How can everyone have just given up when you still don't know anything?' You heard, for instance, about amnesiacs washed up on beaches in the wrong country. And all sorts of people – spies, pop stars, actors – regularly assumed new names and identities. And she didn't want to be morbid, but of course funerals were so important for closure. 'Alice? Do you want to . . . talk about it? About her?'

Alice, balancing on the kitchen stool to reach on top of the cupboards, declined.

'Okay, but I just want to say that you can totally talk to me if you ever feel like it would help.' It was important to leave the channels open. 'I had a cat that disappeared once – Mom said it probably got eaten by the coyotes – and I felt really messed up about that for a long time.' Emily paused. 'Well, obviously that's not exactly a comparable situation.'

'Emily,' said Alice, 'can you hold the stool for me? It keeps wobbling.'

In the thin hours of the early morning the kitchen began to sparkle. Alice stood by the window and looked out into the garden, past the flaming geraniums, to the dark shapes of the trees in the wood and above them the lightening darkness of sky. Low, heavy cumulonimbus clouds had been gathering all night and now they swaddled the sky, muffled the stars. You couldn't make out the Plough, the bright North Star, the shining Belt of Orion. Pausing, broom in hand, Emily stood behind her a moment and followed her gaze into the garden, but though she tried she couldn't see, couldn't see at all, what it was that her cousin's eyes were fixed upon.

On his day off he wandered up the road towards the small parade of shops, past the alleyway that led to the woods, past the entrance to the field by the new housing estate. Spaces that had ceased to be farmland but for some reason or other had never become residential, that were good for children looking for somewhere secret and solitary, for furtive teenagers, for the lonely and the dreamy and the chronically depressed.

He sat for a while at the bus stop playing with the idea of going into town, uncertain because the last time he'd been to the shopping centre security guards had chased him on a suspicion (correct, they would have discovered) that he harboured unpaid-for goods about his person. He liked bus stops because they suggested a favourite fantasy that he was just about to do something wonderful. They always gave him a sense that a different version of his life was within reach and waiting somewhere close by, and that he would be more of a success if only he was there rather than there, here rather than here. Last night, with his face pressed against the wall, which felt clammy with cold, he'd thought that he could hear her moving in the room next door. In the darkness he'd stared sightlessly at the wall, his eyes becoming lasers drilling through cement and brick. But not in a creepy way! Several times the buses approached, slowed down for him, but he raised an arm and waved them on tiredly, regally, a little like a deposed boy-prince come back in disguise to his father's kingdom.

Eventually he got up from the slippery plastic bench and walked on towards the newsagent's. At the end of the alleyway beside the mini-market a man and two women were standing round something on the ground.

'It's really ill,' one of the women said, twisting a magazine in her hands and biting her bottom lip.

'Someone should put it out of its misery,' said the man. The other woman, clinging on to his arm, nodded vigorously.

The pigeon seemed to have a broken wing. It was thin and scrawny and cowered underneath a bush at the edge of the path, occasionally making little jabbing motions with its pigeon head. Its eyes were dull.

'It must be terrified,' said the woman with the magazine. 'Imagine. Surrounded by predators and it can't fly away.'

'Should someone call the RSPCA?' said Danny, looking at the pigeon.

'No point,' said the man, 'this pigeon is almost dead. The kindest thing to do . . .'

'I just don't think I could do it,' said the magazine woman.

'No,' said the girlfriend, 'but you can see that's what it wants.'

The pigeon rooted its head down. It seemed to be staring at Danny with calculating eyes.

'You really think so?'

'Yes, really,' said the man, 'you should do it. Just . . . smash its head.' He looked around. There was a pile of rubble by the side of the path and he picked up a broken brick and handed it to Danny. 'Here, mate. Use this.'

He took the brick. It was a little larger than his fist. He weighed it in his hand.

'I'm not sure about this. I don't really feel comfortable . . . Are you certain – ?'

The women nodded.

'Oh, you just *have* to,' said the magazine woman. They all stepped back. Danny's shadow fell over the pigeon, which made agitated head movements.

'Think of the pain it's in,' whispered the girlfriend behind him.

He shifted the brick from hand to hand. One sharp blow to the head. He crouched down and took a deep breath, lifted the brick over the pigeon's head and brought it down. The sound of feather and flesh mashed into the dirt. Danny dropped the brick and stood back.

'Eww!' said the magazine woman. 'I can't believe you just *did* that.'

'Look,' said the girlfriend, 'you've totally smashed its head in.'

'That's sick,' said the man.

'But –' said Danny.

'You just killed that pigeon,' said the magazine girl.

The three of them drew together and stared at Danny.

'Come on,' said the man coldly, 'let's go.'

He watched them turn away. There was a small splash of pigeon blood on his trousers and a few feathers drifted in the air. Thin, bright red strands, like worms or raw minced beef, came out from the stump of the pigeon's neck. The colour was unnatural, oversimplified, like a child's poster paint.

'But you told me to do it –' he began, and then stopped. Excepting himself and the dead pigeon, the alley was deserted. There was no one to hear him.

A little printed sign had been fixed above the black hole where the balls were rebirthed: DANGER: DO NOT PUT YOUR HANDS IN THE MACHINE. Apparently designers in America were working on a system, based on bowling alley machinery, to transport the plastic trays for keys and wallets at X-ray machines in airports. At the moment those security personnel you saw moving piles of plastic trays were employed *just to do that*. Alice had always sort of assumed that they had other jobs as well and that returning plastic trays was something they did in their downtime.

'I love bowling,' said Emily, pushing back her hair. 'It's important to work out what makes you happy in life.' She unscrewed the cap of her bottle of mineral water and swallowed two small white pills. The other day Emily had left *Choose to be Happy* on Alice's bed with a marker at a section headed 'Why I Hate Myself and Why That's Okay'. She had started saying things like, 'It's fine if you're feeling hostile right now.' Alice sipped from her bottle of Coors and contemplated her feet in the red-and-blue clown-like bowling shoes. She was pleased that Emily was so cheerful. Earlier she'd even gone so far as to eat one or two of Alice's chips, shaking them first to get rid of the salt.

'I mean, everyone has, like, a right to be happy.' *Everyone has a right to be lost.* 'But most people don't know the correct way to go about it. Happiness is like, uh, these bowling pins. It's made out of all these different elements – the separate pins – and if you try to knock them all down together it's difficult, right? But if you knock them down one at a time, suddenly everything becomes a lot more manageable. You should make a little chart with all your happiness goals on it and then work through them.'

'Really? Little charts? Don't you think that happiness is more a by-product of the, er, life well-lived? Still,' Alice picked up a bowling ball and weighed it in her hands, 'I suppose even reaching the point where you're actively looking for happiness must mean that your life is actually going pretty well. In a historical and global sense. You've been able to take time out from worrying about the basics of food production and high maternal mortality rates and –' Her mobile began to ring and she slid the ball down the lane and watched it roll into the gutter as she answered.

'Alice Robinson! My star writer!' It was Tom, calling from the publishing house where he'd finally accepted a job. 'How's life treating you then, Alice? Haven't seen anything of yours in the papers for ages and Peter tells me we've been deserted for the suburbs. Is it true?'

'I guess so,' said Alice. 'I suppose it is.'

'He says he's bringing you a dog later today? I thought you hated dogs? This is not good, Alice, not good at all. Is someone brainwashing you out there? In any case you must be crazed with boredom. Fortunately I don't abandon my staff so easily. This, Alice, is your lucky day. I have a little proposition for you.'

'I'm not really writing at the moment, Tom.'

'No, no, just hear me out. I promise that you'll want to do this. What if I said . . . Karin Ericsson? I need to commission some arty books for our list and I thought of you, of course, and then I thought what would you like most to write about? And then I remembered that you were always on at me about Ericsson, always trying to convince me to commission a piece on her, and I thought, *Perfect!* Alice Robinson on Karin Ericsson.'

'I don't know . . .' Alice looked up at the banks of Americana lights around her. 'I wonder if there's anything new to say? It's been years since she stopped working, and I'm not sure that I'd have anything to add to that big retrospective book the Tate brought out . . . when was that?'

'Six years ago, but okay, okay, I was saving the best till last. When the whole art-book thing came up in a meeting I did think of you straight away but I didn't think of Ericsson until later that week. It turns out that one of the work-experience girls in the office is some sort of distant Ericsson relative – a second cousin, possibly – and off the back of that introduction I've actually been talking with your hyper-reclusive genius and she's offered not just a little thirty-minute interview but, with the right person, with *you*, a whole series of interviews at her place on the coast. I floated the idea that you might even go and stay with her for a bit – really get inside her world . . .'

Emily bowled a strike and squealed.

'Where *are* you, by the way? What's that music?'

'Let me think about it,' said Alice. Tom had always been good at persuading people. 'I'm at a bowling alley right now. I guess I have to go destroy some skittles.'

'Okay, no problem, but don't think too long, Alice. Ericsson is almost certainly the sort of woman who changes her mind about things like this.'

Peter and Isabel arrived in the late afternoon. Alice, watching them from her bedroom window, was pleased to see that they'd left Anka in London to bewail the Polish dockers. Running downstairs she swept piles of junk off the sofa – magazines, jumpers, bags – and opened the front door.

Isabel, dragging the dog behind her and holding a large carpet bag, kissed Alice on both cheeks and squeezed past into the hallway. Peter hesitated on the doorstep and then followed. Alice looked at him and wanted to say something but didn't.

'He's called Selkirk,' said Isabel, indicating the dog.

'Right. Selkirk. Yes,' said Alice. She was staring at the dog. It was so much larger than she'd expected and was standing now, unmoving but tensed, looking at Alice with what seemed a definite if inscrutable hostility. It growled softly, the noise coming up from far inside the deep chest and the black, shaggy fur rising. It had a long, pointed muzzle and roundish amber eyes. The tail, reaching almost down to the floor but then curving upwards at the last moment, twitched once and was still. Alice edged along the sofa a little but Isabel didn't seem to notice. She was explaining Selkirk's dietary requirements.

'I just didn't think he'd be so . . . big,' Alice said, interrupting.

'Yes, he's a real gentle giant,' said Isabel, scratching Selkirk behind the ears. The dog opened its mouth and Alice imagined the gleaming canine teeth sinking into her thigh. 'And he loves being outdoors. I swear he doesn't feel the cold at all. Do you, boy? So you can always just leave him to lope around the garden and he'll be quite happy.

'What did you say? Lope? Isn't that what wolves do?'

'Wolves, dogs, people,' said Peter. 'Anything can lope. Semantics.'

'Right,' said Alice. It looked like a picture she'd seen in a book of folk tales. It looked like the sort of creature that would materialize on a lonely road at night and cause the horses to shy and the coach to overturn. 'Are you staying for supper? I've made fish pie.'

Isabel stared at her. 'Fish pie. Amazing. I just can't believe how . . . domesticated you seem.'

'It's true,' said Alice nodding. 'I even bought a new iron the other day.'

The three were silent a moment contemplating the awesome purchase of an iron, and then Selkirk growled again. 'I think he's hungry,' said Isabel, opening her carpet bag. 'I've brought these biscuits and cans to get you started. And there's a bowl in here somewhere. I'll take him through to the kitchen.'

Peter turned to Alice. 'Are you okay? Did I do something to annoy you? I know that I've been useless at keeping in touch now you're out of London . . .' They looked at each other across the square of beige carpet, which, Alice noticed distractedly, was flecked with

94

crumbs and hairs. There was a sort of high-pitched singing in the silence between them. 'I thought about breaking up with Anka,' he said. 'After the night at the George.' Alice was silent. She knew him too well. She'd already walked all over the island and climbed up to the highest point and seen the sandy beach and the palm trees that grew along the shore in a green fringe. It was utterly familiar; as impossible to claim as to renounce. She was sure he just hadn't realized yet that after a while any sort of relationship would come to feel like a defeat, a making-do. 'Maybe I should still be thinking about that,' Peter said as Isabel and Emily came in.

'We met in the kitchen,' said Isabel. 'I've been explaining Selkirk's diet, how long you need to walk him for, et cetera, et cetera.' She noticed Alice's and Peter's faces and stopped. 'Er, whoops. Have I just – ?'

'Hi, you must be Emily,' said Peter, recovering himself. Emily extracted a hand from the pocket of her skinny jeans and waved.

Besides, Alice continued silently, when she thought of Peter she thought of the city. Walking by the Houses of Parliament on a hot day and feeling the slightly queasy press of humanity. There would be, from the start, no space in their relationship, she worried, nowhere to hide the private parts of themselves. It was something – that complete baring of the self – that should be eased into gradually (like the frog in boiling water). It could be terrible for that to happen all at once.

'Let me help you with the plates,' said Isabel, dragging Alice into the kitchen and opening cupboard doors. 'Are you okay? You looked odd just then. I thought you were ill.' She leaned across the table. 'You didn't tell me that your little cousin was so pretty,' she whispered.

During supper they drank red wine. Isabel put Selkirk out in the garden and Alice could see his dark shape moving beyond the window glass. He looked happy enough out there in the blackness opening and closing his hot red mouth.

'Dogs were shunned in many ancient cultures,' Alice said. 'They were seen as *not right* because they straddled both the animal and human worlds, which was considered a definition of monstrousness.'

She'd found all the candles in the house – small, round scented ones, the plain white sticks that her parents kept stocked against power cuts, tall red Christmas candles – and ranged them across the table and along the mantelpiece. They softened everyone's faces and the warm glow merged with the warm glow of the wine until everything in the room was gently swimming.

Peter got up and began wandering around the room, peering at the family photographs hung over the sideboard. He pointed to one of Alice in her Girl Guide uniform and saluted. 'I always forget, Alice, about these rather fascist tendencies of yours. Dib, dib, dib; dob, dob, dob. I can't really imagine you as a Girl Guide though. I thought the only time you'd been camping was at a festival.' He sat back down. 'So, did you hear that the shop by the canal has started putting your groceries into vintage-style brown paper bags with no handles? Totally retrogressive behaviour.'

'I sort of like it . . .' said Isabel. 'It makes me feel as though I'm in a Hollywood romcom. You know, I'm walking along clutching the bag to my chest and can hardly see over the top . . .'

'And so of course you stumble . . .'

'And so of course I stumble and bang, the groceries are all over the floor, but then some handsome young man appears to pick up my organic aubergines and . . .'

'It's amazingly dumb,' said Peter, shaking his head.

Emily turned to Isabel. 'I love your hair. That's how I want to have my hair one day. I mean, like, when I'm much older, when I'm starting to look *mature*?'

'Thank you, Emily.' Isabel raised her eyebrows and then turned to Alice across the table. 'You must go see the new exhibition at the Williams gallery.' She emptied her glass. 'You've looked at those pictures before in magazines and such, but really, up close the colours just *glow*.' She upended the wine bottle. 'Oh. Are we out of drink? Should I run and get some more wine?'

'We're not in Kansas any more,' said Alice. 'They don't do after-hours off-licences out here.'

Isabel made a small moue of shock. 'Now that is just uncivilized.'

'I think there might be some sherry.'

'Goodie, I actually like sherry. And it will be good training for when we get old and move to the coast.'

'And eat fish and chips every day . . .'

'And wave at the young men on the beach . . .'

'And have thousands of cats and – wait, isn't Johnny coming?'

Isabel lowered her voice. 'Everyone knows that men die younger. I'm thinking we'll just be two crazy old women together.'

Out of the corner of her eye Alice watched Emily asking Peter about being a journalist. She leaned towards him over the remains of the fish pie.

'But there's no work in London,' Peter was saying. He looked depressed for a moment.

'But you're really smart,' said Emily. 'I'm sure there must be like hundreds of people wanting to employ you.'

'You'd think.'

She nodded sympathetically. 'Maybe you need to, I don't know, look at a different town or something. It's really important to stay proactive, isn't it?'

Peter gestured with his knife. 'That's actually a pretty good thought. I've got an idea for a book, but I've been thinking that I maybe need a change of scene to get started. I think I could write it if I was somewhere else. Paris, Berlin.'

They both reached for the pepper at the same time and their hands brushed slightly.

'Tom phoned earlier. He wants me to write a book for him about Karin Ericsson,' Alice said to Isabel.

'See?' said Peter, pointing a finger at Alice as he tried to focus across the table. 'Those are the people taking all my jobs.'

'Seriously. Shall I do it?'

'Didn't that big Tate book come out when she died?'

'Nope – she didn't die. Where did you hear that? Turns out she's become some sort of seaside recluse. Tom's going to fix up an interview if I say yes.'

'But of course you must do it!' said Isabel. 'She's one of your favourite artists. And think about the money. I mean, I know everyone was sad about *Meta* and I know you've had,' she indicated Emily with a small head movement, 'stuff to sort out, but you haven't worked for ages. It's so strange that she's not dead. Don't you think it's strange? I still have a postcard of one of her paintings that you sent me from Paris.' She hiccoughed. 'So where's the sherry?'

Alice stood up and started stacking the dirty plates. 'I wasn't planning on writing anything for a while, but you know how persuasive Tom can be. I said I'd think about it.' She had reached that stage of drunkenness where she seemed always to be watching herself in a darkly lit film, with every gesture ennobled by the gaze of the camera. Walking slowly towards the kitchen she glanced at her reflection in the hall mirror. Red wine stains arched up from the corners of her mouth, getting caught in the two lines that ran down on either side between her nose and lips.

In the kitchen she began assembling the pudding. She'd made one of her mother's recipes – *îles flottantes*, floating islands. On each plate a soft white ball of beaten egg-whites and sugar, a sort of poached meringue, floated in its personal lake of vanilla custard. In a saucepan she heated sugar and water to make caramel, watching the sugar dissolve into a sweet sauce, and then, while she waited for the mixture to cool slightly, she switched on the radio and rolled a cigarette. A woman was singing something sad and plaintive in a foreign language. Alice wandered back into the hall and stood in front of the mirror.

You look like the Joker, said Janey, standing beside her in the glass. *I think she was right. I think you need to moisturize more.* She flicked her long blonde hair. Alice sniffed. If she concentrated she thought that she could smell the smoke rising from the cigarette that Janey was holding in her hand.

In the kitchen she used a fork to drizzle strands of caramel over the wobbly poached island and added flakes of dried almond. She could hear Peter and Isabel laughing in the next room and then stopping.

'Emily!' she called. 'Can you come help carry?'

'Did you know that in a crematorium the average human body turns to dust in just ninety minutes?' Sandra led them briskly through the corridors of the Lighthouse Nursing Home. 'Whereas in soil of neutral acidity your bones can last for centuries.' She opened the double fire-retardant doors and ushered them past the picture gallery. 'Hundreds of years. Just think of it!'

Emily hoped that this particular nurse wouldn't be on duty the next time they visited. The sound of an unseen vacuum cleaner played down the corridor. Sandra stopped in front of a closed room. 'Excuse me one moment?' She pushed the door open, and beyond was a smiling woman sitting up in bed with a peach-coloured shawl around her shoulders. 'Time for your sweeties, Lorna,' she said, taking a handful of coloured tablets from the bedside table. She leaned over and with one swift motion pushed back the woman's head and pressed the pills between her lips, holding her chin up until she swallowed. 'Good girl,' she said. The woman smiled serenely.

'Lorna,' said Sandra as they continued down the corridor. 'Her husband died last week and her daughter wanted to know whether we should tell her, but I said, "What's the point? She won't understand you." They'd been married seventy-two years, if you can conceive of that at your ages, and never spent a night apart until she deteriorated, her mind deteriorated, so much that she had to come, what was left of her, here to us. And what is the point, you may wonder, of seventy-two years of marriage that end like this? Look how happy and content she is and yet she couldn't even tell you his name. Seventy-two years of marriage.

If she'd known it was going to end like this, would she have bothered?'

Sandra smoothed back her hair and flung open the doors to the day room. 'You'll see yourselves from here? I have to talk about shifts with the cleaning staff. Some unauthorized alterations to the rota have been brought to my attention.'

Mrs Austin was sitting in the same straight-backed chair by the window, sewing. 'Which is all very well,' she said to Alice, 'which is an important life skill that I suspect many young people today to be without, but it does become a little tiresome after a while. Also, I've been undertaking some birdwatching' – she had a pair of binoculars on her lap – 'three blackbirds and two robins this afternoon.' She sighed. 'It lacks excitement. Did I tell you about the time I caught a burglar at the Vicarage? Tied him up with six inches of string. That's a trick worth knowing.' Her eyes gleamed. 'I've sometimes thought of tying that nurse up with six inches of string. Has she talked to you about funerals yet? I used to think she was running some sort of racket with the local undertaker's, but lately I've decided that there's a more fanatic edge to it. She has a decidedly morbid personality. Still, never lose your temper with an adversary, Alice. If you are in the right there's no need to; if you are in the wrong you can't afford to.'

Emily, wandering over to the window, was accosted by the small woman in the pink cardigan. 'But I already told you,' she said frustratedly, 'I don't have any butter.'

Around her she was aware that the other residents were starting to become restless. There were four women and two men lined up on chairs like shy children at a birthday party and, one by one, they began to moan, to bang softly on the floor with their walking sticks, to make sharp, agitated movements with their heads. Escaping the pink-cardiganned woman, Emily came over to where Alice and Mrs Austin sat. 'Are they all right? Is something upsetting them?'

Mrs Austin looked around and then glanced out of the window. 'It's the time of day. They always get like this when the sun is setting. The staff here call it "sundowning". I think perhaps it has to do with memories of leaving work, going home and so forth. Around this time they instinctively feel that they should be doing something, going somewhere. They'll calm down presently, but you might turn the light on over there – that sometimes helps.'

Emily nodded and walked across to the light switch. Manoeuvring around a wheelchair, she knocked the blanket off the legs of its occupant, an elderly man with watery, pale blue eyes. 'Hoi!' He suddenly sprung to life. 'Are you one of the nurses? I've been waiting hours.' He waved angrily towards his crotch, where a dark patch was spreading across the grey material of his sweatpants. Emily wrinkled her nose and the man laughed. 'You're too pretty to be one of them, aren't you, sweetheart?' He leered upwards. 'Maybe *you* could clean me up? Give me a sponge bath? Hmmm? I promise to behave myself.' He winked and rubbed his knotted hands up and down his thighs.

Trying to be a good person was difficult, Emily thought, backing away from the wheelchair. Plus, there was just something really icky about old people. Even the unperverted ones.

'Oh dear. Had a little accident, Albert?' Sandra appeared suddenly between them, making Emily start. Albert was silent. 'Waiting for hours? Such nonsense. Such a storyteller.' She shook her head cheerfully and turned to Emily, looking down at her. 'We must make allowances for the residents here; we must always consider their time of life, what they are facing. I do my best to help prepare them, but I'm afraid that some, your friend Margery for instance, find contemplation difficult. I hope you take the time to consider such matters yourself.' She patted Emily's head. 'After all, we're never too young. What was it Keats said? Life is a fragile dewdrop on a perilous journey. Something like that.'

I'm so never coming here again, thought Emily. She decided that later she'd have a long bath and deep-condition her hair. That was always relaxing.

Part Three

'Girls can even be brave enough to shoot tigers, if they can keep cool.'

How Girls Can Help to Build Up the Empire: The Handbook for Girl Guides
(1912)

The spring was still at an indeterminate stage with the greenness only starting vaguely here and there, and sometimes Alice caught a sense of vertigo, of not knowing which season she was in, of what was ahead of her.

Winter had not been good for the house. You could see that now in the new light. Decaying leaves were banked around the outer walls so it looked as though the building had risen up from underneath the vegetable matter, like a burrowing animal coming out of the earth and leaving behind a conical mound of soil. The paint on the door and on the eaves was flaking a little and the windows were smeary with grease from where Alice and Emily had rested their heads, their hands, embayed, staring out at the unchanging street. The garden, at first kept in check by the winter frosts, was turning rampant. Already the ornamental pond was choked with mulch so that it no longer reflected the sky.

Emily had been enrolled at the local secondary school for the spring term and back at home, trying on her uniform, she stood horrified in front of the mirror, plucking at the heavy grey skirt, at the unflattering length of it. The blazer was a sexless royal blue and boxy thing. The tie strangled her.

'I have to go outside in this?' she said. 'These are just *so* not my colours. Are you sure people actually *wear* this stuff?'

'Yup,' said Alice. 'School uniform teaches us from a young age that individuality is a great confidence trick.' She patted the pockets of her jeans, looking for her cigarette papers. 'Everybody wears the school uniform. No special dispensations.'

'Whatever.' Emily concentrated on trying to roll up the waistband of her skirt. 'Can I borrow those shoes?' She indicated Janey's faux crocodile-skin heels, six-inch things with complicated straps.

'Those are not shoes,' said Alice, staring at them. 'Those are an attempt to label you a socially constructed woman as opposed to merely a born one.'

'So can I wear them or what?'

'No. You won't be able to walk. And I'm sure the school has rules about heels. They did when I was there.'

Emily pouted.

Alice picked up the shoes. She remembered Janey buying them in town and wearing them to an end-of-term disco. Was it strange the way her parents had kept all of Janey's belongings waiting for her? Or was that normal? There had just never been a moment when it felt appropriate to put everything away, send the clothes to Oxfam, and a year had become two, four, ten, seventeen, and Janey's room had waited like a time capsule and no one had wanted to be the first to say anything about it.

'The black shoes you have look great,' she said to Emily. 'Honestly.' She took Janey's platforms with her when she left.

Later, watching her cousin walk off towards the bus stop, Alice was surprised by an anxious feeling, a nagging impotence and concern. She made coffee and toast in the dirty kitchen and scrolled through her emails. There was a gossiping message from Isabel about people who already seemed too far away, like half-watched characters in a television soap. An invitation to the private view of Johnny's next show; more of his increasingly beautiful, melancholy pen-and-ink sketches showing what looked like the aftermaths of natural disasters. Another message from Tom chasing up the Ericsson project. *Had she come to a decision?* She hadn't.

Isabel's parents seemed in no particular hurry to take Selkirk away to dog-heaven Hampshire, and now his food bowl was filled again with hard, autumnal-coloured biscuits shaped like tiny bones and smelling unpleasantly of pet shops. Perhaps she was guilty of overfeeding but it seemed safer: she didn't want hunger to awaken any primal killing instincts and she didn't trust him to rationality. She didn't understand the animal longings in his eyes. She didn't trust him not to decide, for some incomprehensible animal reason, to snap at her unprotected calf as she edged by him towards the back door where her boots waited. It would be better if Selkirk were one of those charming, silly dogs that chased snowflakes and plastic bags and, perhaps, their own excitable tails, but he was too dignified for that, never appearing to experience what would anthropomorphically be called 'fun'. Outside, plenty of small, soft, furry things had been chased, but if there was enjoyment to be had it seemed to come from the feel of his own powerful body, from the crush of canine teeth, from the squirming softness bloodied between his jaws. There was no space for humour in Selkirk's world.

They walked through the enclosed woodland behind the house towards where the interwar semis were replaced by a honeycomb-coloured 1960s housing estate that represented the farthest spread of the suburb. From the small, PVC-framed windows of the houses and flats, blossom trees and forsythia bushes could be seen, but still the greenness of the estate and the small recreation ground that lay between the houses and the woods never felt quite like nature but more like dead space. Alice hadn't been back since returning from London, though the summer of Janey's disappearance she'd spent hours walking over the grass in the hot sunshine, first convinced that there would be something the police had missed, and later simply taking comfort from being in that final place, the last physical link between the world and her sister. A small splash of blue vanishing, vanishing, gone. It felt different now, in the damp spring: blander and less mysterious.

Janey, according to the story the police put together, finished school at three thirty and walked with Amanda Rowe to the house of Nicola Perry. They ate supper there – fish fingers, boiled potatoes, peas – and watched television. At around seven fifteen the three girls walked up to the parade and bought ice creams. (The newsagent confirmed the purchase from till receipts: two chocolate, one strawberry.) Amanda left at that point to go home (she had promised to look after her younger brother) and the other two continued on to the recreation ground by the woods. It was approximately half past seven. They sat on a bench and, presumably, chatted (about boys, about exams, about nothing). Janey, who loved animals, threw sticks for a dog that was nosing around without its owner. The last time that Nicola saw Janey was at ten past eight (she'd looked at her watch because, she said, she was going to be late home). She and Janey lived in opposite directions so they didn't leave together. The sky was still blue though the air had cooled. The air smelled of fresh green things. It was early summer.

A dog walker reported seeing a blonde girl in the blue St Anne's uniform sitting alone in the recreation ground at eight twenty. At eight thirty Alice said that she thought Janey had gone to see Martin. Her mother said, 'I hope she doesn't stay out too late. It's a school night, after all.' At eight forty-five the quality of the light was changing, the edges of all the shapes were blurring slightly. The sky was still blue but the shadowed parts of the world were darker. A woman looking out of the back window of her house saw a girl with blonde hair wearing a blue uniform walking slowly along the strip of path by the woods, smoking a cigarette. She watched, she said, because the girl's head was so bright against the darkness of the trees. That was the last sighting, a small splash of blue picking its way along the nowhere strip of land between the honeycomb-coloured houses and the darkening woods, receding, already, into the flatness of memory.

Alice started from her reverie. Selkirk, his tongue hanging out like a piece of cooked ham, was standing over a small white dog. It cringed and whimpered. Alice stared at Selkirk hopelessly. 'Do you have to be so *confrontational*?' There was no lead. Selkirk hated to wear a lead. (She had long ago stopped trying to explain this to the clockwork dog walkers whose animals he menaced.)

The owner of the white dog hurried towards them, lips pursing around a curse or admonition, but then, seeing Alice, he smiled. 'Alice!' he said. He sounded pleased.

'Martin!' said Alice, grinning through slightly clenched teeth. She waved her arms ineffectually at Selkirk, who ignored her. 'The dogs –'

The small white dog crawled out from under Selkirk's nose towards Martin, who crouched down and clipped a lead on to its collar. 'Good to see you again, Alice. Wow' – he stared admiringly at Selkirk – 'how does he fit into the city?'

He fell in to step beside her so that they walked together past the burned remains of the old picnic bench towards the children's playground.

'He's not mine really. I'm looking after him for a friend. Just while I'm down here.'

'Friends.' Martin pushed back thinning hair. 'I used to have some of those. Now I have a dog.' He made his face go tragic for a moment.

'What about' – oh, she was bad with names – 'your wife?'

'Divorced. Actually, I think I may have misled you a little before. I was embarrassed. It was a weird impulse to make me seem like a bit less of a failure.' He looked sideways at her. 'Don't hate me?'

'Oh. Well. Of course not. I'm sorry about the divorce.'

They walked on a few more paces in silence. He loomed above her with his large hands hanging down and swinging like Frankenstein's Monster.

'By the way, might be best to put the dog back on his lead now. He looks like he could be a bit boisterous with all the kiddies running around over there.'

'I don't have one; he doesn't respond well to them. He's, er, surprisingly gentle though. He'd never attack anyone.' She hoped this was true.

'Right. Cool. So do you want to meet my little girl? Ruby. A neighbour's keeping an eye on her in the playground. On Saturdays I do the whole divorced-dad thing. You know, McDonald's, the park, guilt presents.'

They'd reached the swings. The old gravel that worked its way so painfully into skinned knees had been replaced by a soft, black rubberized surface and the only playground equipment was a small, brightly coloured 'play centre' in the shape of a ship. Before, there had been a tall, rackety slide and a complicated climbing frame of bare metal burnished by hundreds of tiny hands. When she was small, Janey, who tended to get overexcited about things, had only been allowed on the slide with her older sister. Alice remembered feeling the wriggling, sticky hand in hers as she tried not to look between the metal rungs of the ladder at the earth so far below.

'Interesting fact,' said Alice. 'Despite new safety standards in playgrounds, children's injury levels have remained absolutely constant; they simply find more dangerous things to do on the safer equipment.'

Martin waved to a tired-looking woman pushing a toddler on the swings. 'That's my neighbour.' Then he pointed out a small girl with gingerish hair and a pink nose. She was crouched with a darker, slender-faced friend, digging in the earth near the litter bin.

'No, this is the bedroom,' said the gingerish child bossily. 'No it *is*.'

'He's been naughty,' said the slender-faced one. 'He has to go to bed. Bad boy. Bad, bad boy. Smack him.'

'Mummy's in the kitchen. She's making . . . cake.'

'No cake for him.'

'Mummy will eat all the cake.'

'Yes. Mummy will eat all the cake.'

'*Bad* boy.'

The gingerish girl looked up and, without saying goodbye to her friend, ran over to her father. Martin bent down to scoop her up. 'Hello, munchkin!' He hoisted the girl on to his shoulders and turned back to Alice. 'I want you to meet Daddy's friend. This is Alice.' The girl scowled darkly before hiding her face in Martin's hair. He laughed and put her down. 'She's shy with strangers. Aren't you, Ruby? Look,' turning to Alice, 'I hope this doesn't seem weird, but I was thinking maybe we could go for a drink sometime?'

'That would be nice,' said Alice. It did seem weird, but what were you supposed to say to a man holding the hand of a four-year-old? She didn't want to give the child some sort of rejection complex.

She sat on the bench by the playground, the unburned one, and watched them walk away towards the car park, the big hand holding the little, the white dog trotting at their heels. Overhead the sky was grey. On the litter bin was a sign: LOVE YOUR STREETS: BIN YOUR LITTER. The usefulness of Love was overrated, Alice thought, and these days it seemed to get into everything. Love was a sort of twisted way of going about things because it suggested always the possibility of not-Love. It suggested that whatever was being proffered because of Love (litter-binning, a parent's care, spiritual salvation) might capriciously be withdrawn at any moment. Better, she thought, a moral or legal obligation. One might know where one was with that.

Alice read the message again: Peter was engaged. It was inconceivable, she realized, for Peter to be engaged. Only in some alternative universe where she and he and everyone they knew had been replaced by alien life forms could Peter be engaged. She lay down on her bed, staring at the pink and lavender wallpaper, and heard the front door open and close and Emily's footsteps in the hallway.

I can't believe you're going on a date with my ex, said Janey, interrupting her musings. *That's totally messed up.* Janey was sitting on the desk next to the laptop and cleaning the dirt from underneath her nails with a pair of scissors. Alice shrugged with more nonchalance than she felt. 'You always argued. It wouldn't have lasted. I'm bored. Also, not to piss you off or anything, but you're not really here, are you? You're not about to date him again.' *That*, said Janey, *is so not the point.* She narrowed her eyes. *You can't just forget about me. You can't just pretend I never happened.*

She could, perhaps, pretend that the email had never happened. She could wrap it up in black cloth and put it in a box of things never to be talked about again, things never to be picked up and dusted off and displayed on a mantelpiece for visitors to see. Maybe it would all work out fine.

There was a knock at the door and Emily came in and then stopped and looked confused. 'Sorry, I thought you were on the phone.' She perched on the edge of the bed, picked up Alice's hairbrush and began smoothing down her hair. She looked so much younger without any make-up and in the neatly pleated grey skirt, pale blue blouse and royal blue blazer, and it was always rather miraculous to see her emerge each morning from the chaotic house looking so serious and well scrubbed.

'Good day?'

Emily shook her head. 'The day pretty much sucked. Kara – you know that girl I was telling you about – we had to partner in double science and she just goes on and on about her brother, Luke, like he's the coolest thing ever or something. It's so amazingly dull. Luke, Luke, Luke.'

'I thought Kara was your new best friend?'

'Ha! Yeah right. She is so totally self-involved. And she always has to be in charge of everything we do. She bosses Laura and Anita around the whole time and they don't even say anything.'

Emily reached over to Alice and touched her hair. 'You need a trim.' She began working with the brush. 'In fact, when did you last wash this at all?'

Alice shrugged, wincing as Emily snagged a tangle.

'So don't take this the wrong way, but when you went out earlier? You didn't look like this? I mean you'd gotten dressed, right?'

'I am dressed.' Alice looked down at herself. It was true that she was wearing a pair of pyjama bottoms, but they were thick, towelling ones. Sweatpants almost. She also had on a large V-necked cable-knit cardigan covered in dog hairs with a hole in one elbow, and, yes, now she looked at it, there was some sort of food that had trickled down the front and congealed.

'Well, I had a coat on,' she said, wiggling her feet. 'Are you hungry?'

Alice had given up cooking on a regular basis. They'd started eating a lot of cereal, and Emily nibbled handfuls of nuts and sunflower seeds and dried seaweed. She refused the processed white bread, chocolate biscuits and plastic-tasting full-fat Cheddar cheese that Alice brought home from sporadic shopping trips.

'Not really, but we should go to the supermarket soon,' said Emily. 'I want to get some miso soup and I really need some decent shampoo and conditioner. That stuff you buy is just stripping my hair.' She grabbed a length of blonde in her hand and waved it at Alice. 'See how many split ends? I'm going to have to cut a whole bunch off.' She put the hairbrush down and removed a Pre-Stress supplement from her blazer pocket and dry-swallowed it.

'You want to go shopping now?'

'No thanks, I need to get ready for the school party.' She studied her fingernails. 'By the way, what's the boy next door called? I keep seeing him around. Is he nice? He's kind of strange-looking.'

'He's called Daniel. I think they threw him out of the sixth form for something. Drugs? Theft? It's the sort of thing my mother would know.'

'Uh huh. Okay. Hey, aren't you going on your date tonight?'

'Yes. So?'

'So you, like, need to get ready too?'

'I'm thirty-four. It doesn't take me three hours to get ready for a date any more.'

Emily shook her head. 'Well, I think it's so awesome that you're still dating anyhow. It's great that you're still out there.' She smiled and went upstairs to run a bath.

'Thanks,' said Alice to the empty doorway. 'Cheers.' She tossed the hairbrush in the air but failed to catch it and it clunked against the back of her head.

Emily left for her party and sometime after that a wind got up. Selkirk seemed unusually restless, pacing up and down and growling to himself in that softly, softly menacing way, refusing to be distracted from whatever it was that agitated him. Alice remembered that according to Burke we love dogs because they're weaker than us and because we control them, but Selkirk was a compulsively independent animal. Alice poured out his food but it was only when she turned away that he would consent to begin eating, his dependence on her clearly a cruel humiliation. She fed him now, while in the garden the wind whipped the branches of the apple tree and pulled the hydrangeas into fantastical contortions. The black plastic dustbin by the garage clattered over and the lid flew past the kitchen window like a miniature UFO late for some intergalactic space meeting. She turned on the radio and listened to the newsreader talk of job cuts, of Depression-era levels of unemployment.

The phone rang and when she answered it was Isabel calling in a state of some excitement. 'Alice! Peter getting married! Can you believe it?'

'I know . . . I sort of can't.'

'I'm so pleased for him.'

'Yes. Of course. Don't you think she's a bit young though?'

'I saw them yesterday and they look very sweet together actually. Very nuptial.'

'It just seems so sudden. Do you think she's pregnant?'

'Wouldn't that be a rather recherché reason for a wedding? And anyway no, I don't think she's pregnant; they haven't set a date yet. But how are *you*, Alice? When are you coming back? I mean, aren't you worried that everything is sort of carrying on without you here? Johnny says that there's this girl, Lucy something or other, who's been covering lots of your old slots . . . But I guess you have a plan. There's the book, isn't there? That sounded like a good thing. Johnny said people are excited about the book.'

'Mmm. Perhaps . . .' She appreciated Isabel's concern, but only in a vague, detached sort of way.

'Maybe you've got that . . . what's the thing that hermits used to get in the desert? Acid . . . Acidity . . .'

'Accidie. Spiritual or mental sloth.' *Accidie: the tedium or perturbation of the heart. A state akin to dejection.*

'Yes, so – oh, hold on, is that the time? Sorry – just realized I'm late for this film screening at London Bridge. Talk later?'

'Sure – go, go. We'll talk another time.'

'Bye, Alice.'

'Bye. Love to Johnny.'

Alice stared at the phone. Weddings. Babies. *Women can't wait as long as men, Alice.* She and Isabel had spent their twenties talking about the value of time spent living alone. They'd rather looked down on girls who had serial relationships; it seemed a little, what, *weak*? And then, Alice thought, you suddenly began to wonder. Over time you began to suspect that life was not, in fact, a college course designed to foster personal growth. You began to wonder whether those serial daters had understood something you had failed to see.

The clock in the dining room rang the half-hour; she went to the front door, opened it and peered out. The wind was gusting so strongly now that it had become almost solid, leanable. Little pieces of grit swirled on the porch and the hydrangeas bent forwards and prostrated themselves against the soil, their mop-like, sterile heads all ghostly in the early evening dark. There was a terrific crash and Alice jumped and shrieked as a tile, launched from the roof, suddenly smashed beside her feet. Her heart jolted like she'd missed a step on a flight of stairs; a sickening, second-long intimation of free-fall. She nudged the shattered tile with her toe, shivered and stepped backwards. 'Janey?' she said. 'I think I almost died.'

'Good day?' he asked while they idled at the traffic lights.

'Mmm. Thanks. Just, you know, at home reading and stuff.'

'Oh yes? Can't say that I'm much of a reader myself. All that stuff they gave us at school put me off.'

The lights changed and Martin pulled away with a burst of engine noise. She was thinking that Peter was one of the few people she knew with a book collection larger than her own – but she wasn't going to think about Peter.

'This is fun,' she said. 'I hardly know anyone in the city with a car.'

Martin grinned. 'You need a vehicle out here,' he said.

Near the town centre they drove past the shopping arcade to the multi-storey that smelled, always, somehow greasy. Martin parked at the top, in the open air, and when they'd climbed out they kept back from the edge because the wind was still blowing so strongly. Lighted cars crawled along the roads far beneath them. Alice moved forwards to get a better view. 'It makes me think of *The Third Man*. You know, "And would you really feel any pity if one of those dots stopped moving for ever?"'

Martin shook his head. 'It's too windy, Alice. Don't get so close to the edge.'

'Look!' she said, pointing. 'There's our old school. And the clock tower. I don't remember the clock tower being lit up like that.'

'Alice!'

She turned and suddenly Martin had moved up very close and she was struck again by quite how much of Martin there was and she leaned back away from him over the parapet.

'You're making me nervous,' he said. 'Come back from the edge now.'

Martin led the way to a high-ceilinged place that had previously been a bank and had quotations from Oscar Wilde stencilled across its walls. She noticed that there was a tiny rectangle of pink-beige plaster taped to the inside of his arm over that thin, delicate patch of skin where the veins and arteries show through. She pointed with her unlit roll-up. 'What did you do?'

'Where? This? Nothing.' He ripped away the Elastoplast. 'I gave blood yesterday and forgot to take off the plaster.' There was a minuscule red pinprick on the white skin. 'Listen, I know you probably don't want to talk about this, not with me, but I wanted you to know that I still think about her.'

'Okay.'

'I just always got the impression you thought I didn't care.'

Alice remained silent.

'I still want to know what happened, why she ran away,' he said.

'You think that's what she did?'

'It's what we have to hope, isn't it?'

The wine glass was tall and slippery between her hands. She looked at Martin. 'I suppose people can get overheated at that age. Things – loves, relationships, infidelities – can seem more important than they are.'

Martin blushed. 'I was so scared the first night that the police pulled me in for questioning and I hadn't even seen her that day. I felt so guilty.' He fumbled. 'I mean, guilty because I hadn't . . . been able to stop it. Whatever it was. Hadn't protected her. Not, you know . . .'

'Actually' – she took a gulp of wine – 'do you mind if we stop doing this? I just don't think that I want to have this conversation right now.'

'Sorry. Of course.' He stared at his hands as though they might suggest a better topic for discussion, as though his brain had temporarily ceded control to his Marlboro-stained fingertips. 'So are you going away this summer? Any holiday plans?'

'Not yet. I'm going to the coast at some point though to stay with an artist I'm writing about. A book, probably.'

Martin nodded. 'You always were smart,' he said. 'Writing books.' He smiled and then suddenly, as if he'd been waiting for that precise moment all evening, lunged with his hand and dropped it heavily on to Alice's knee. They both stared at the hand for a moment.

Alice coughed. 'New scientific research suggests that our brains decide to perform an action a whole ten seconds before we consciously realize it. I definitely find that spooky. It's an idea . . . that we're led by our bodies rather than by what you might call our conscious minds . . . it's as if there's no such thing as self-determination or free will.'

'Oh,' he said, taking back his hand.

Alice clutched her wine glass. Why was a wine glass always empty when you needed it? 'Would you like another drink? Shall we drink some Scotch?' She hunted through her bag for her wallet. 'Or should you have a soft drink? Does giving blood cancel out the fact that you drink-drive?' She studied her own hands. She'd allowed Emily to paint her nails and they were, it struck her now, the colour of the fingernails of dead girls in body bags on made-for-TV dramas. 'It's very careless of you.'

'I know my limit,' he said, frowning. 'I know what's too much.'

On the doorstep he smiled hopefully. The car keys jangled in his hand as she vacillated. He looked down and saw the broken tile.

'Ouch! When did this happen?' Nudging it with his foot.

'Earlier today. This wind,' she said, making up her mind. 'Well, thanks again for the lift. Good night.' Closing the door at last and thinking, *Amazing that Janey would now be over thirty. Impossible that Janey should be so old.* The house was silent and she checked the time: eleven fifteen. Selkirk slunk into the hallway and stared at her for a moment as if verifying her identity, and then retreated to the kitchen. She dialled Emily's number.

'Hey, yeah, I'm just walking home. I'm at the top of the street. Be there in five.'

Still without turning on the lights Alice stood by the living-room window and watched the wind-whipped hydrangeas in the garden, the colourless lawn. *What am I doing here?* She felt panicked for a moment, standing and watching as everything she'd worked for sauntered carelessly away down the road. She imagined herself as a mad old lady running up to strangers in the street. *Do you know who I am? People used to listen to me. My opinions mattered.* They looked at her with bemused distaste.

Eventually Emily appeared in the distance walking down the hill. Her hair looked silvery instead of gold, bobbing up and down in time to whatever was playing on her iPod. A little way behind her was a tall, thin figure. It was hard to be certain but it seemed as though he slowed down whenever Emily did, dipped in and out of the shadows of the parked cars like some noirish gumshoe, but then he stopped and abruptly turned away up the crescent on the left and disappeared from sight, leaving Emily alone on the pavement by the house. Alice frowned and went to open the front door.

Eight times out of ten the customer would have said, if made to answer honestly, that they would have preferred for you to be a machine, something there was no need to interact with beyond the passing over of a card, the tapping out of some numbers. Mostly Danny was fine with that. Mostly he was used to a detached sort of relationship with other people: behind glass, distant and far away as though he were still living quietly underneath the thick grey ice on the lake. He was disappointed, though, that his manager, Paul, remained wary of him even though his till had never been down and even though he'd dutifully learned which wines to recommend with which meats and fish. After a probation period employees were sent for a day's wine tasting at the company headquarters near London Bridge, but so far Paul had been entirely silent on that matter. Danny thought that he might have mentioned it in passing at least. According to Nick, the deputy manager, most people were sent for training after the third week.

On the credit side of things the off-licence was often quiet and then it was possible simply to sit and read and be paid for that. He had with him now *When the Greenhouse Floods* – he tried to keep up an interest – and had already learned that fairly soon a number of islands in the South Seas would be completely submerged. The bell on the door rang and four girls came in, clattering all over the floor in their heels until it sounded as though they walked on hooves. The tallest – the only one making eye contact with him – grabbed a pack of beers and a bottle of vodka and slammed them on to the counter.

'Pack of Marlboro Lights. Twenty. Please.'

Danny mumbled and pulled at his brown quiff.

'Pardon?'

He repeated himself. 'ID? For the vodka? The beer?'

She swayed forwards until he could smell perfume and the minty chewing gum on her breath. 'But I'm twenty-one. Can't you see? I've been eighteen for years.'

He looked down, found her cleavage and jerked his head back up again.

She folded her arms. 'So, ah, are you seriously not going to serve me? I left my ID, my driving licence . . . in the car.'

'Can you get it?' Almost whispered. His hand was doing it again, unconsciously pulling and tugging at the hank of hair in front of his left eye. He forced his hand down on to the counter where it lay like a large, dead, white spider. 'I'm just doing my job . . .' How amazingly pathetic he sounded.

'But I'm parked miles away. I –' She stopped suddenly and smiled at him. 'Come on. You know I'm over eighteen. Please? Just this once? I'll bring my ID next time but we're going to be late for the party and it's her birthday.' She jerked her thumb back towards the fourth girl, who was loitering near the door and who turned round, surprised. 'We need something to celebrate with, don't we? Emily?'

'Huh? I mean, yep. Yes we do.' Blushing, she began to study her painted toenails but when, a few moments later, she looked back up her face was blank. She narrowed her eyes.

'Okay,' he said quickly, 'okay.' He made his voice sound stern. 'But you definitely need to bring some ID next time.'

'Oh God, yeah, absolutely,' said the tall girl, nodding enthusiastically and passing two twenty-pound notes across the counter. 'You're just a complete life-saver.'

Danny rang through the purchases, handed her the change and put the drinks and cigarettes into a carrier bag. The four of them turned on their heels, synchronized like dancers, and Emily opened the shop door.

'Have a good party!' he called after them, smiling.

They paused with the door half open and the tall girl turned round to stare at him. She curled her lip. 'Yeah' – she turned back to her companions – 'whatever' – and they burst out laughing as they disappeared into the street.

He stood for a while with the end of his grin still hanging, unwanted, around the corners of his mouth.

Paul arrived at ten and went straight through to the back room. Danny served one more customer – it was another slow night – and then it was ten thirty and he turned the sign on the door to 'closed' and began cashing up. Paul came out.

'Dan. Any problems tonight?'

'No.'

'Any difficult customers?'

'No.'

'Quiet, was it?'

'Yes.'

'Not rushed off your feet? Not too busy to think?'

'No.'

'Okay. Right.' Paul leaned back against the counter with his arms folded. 'So why, when I'm going through the security tapes, do I see you selling alcohol to underage kids?'

'What?' Danny stopped with the till open and a bunch of twenties in his hand. 'I didn't. I don't know –'

'Those four girls who came in?'

'Oh. *Them.*' The notes crinkled in his hand. 'They were twenty-one. I asked them.'

Paul leaned over, pulled the notes from his hand and put them back in the till. 'Danny, a) they don't look twenty-one; they look sixteen; b) I just told you I watched the security tape. I know that you didn't see any ID from them; c) I also happen to know that they're not twenty-one because they're all in my daughter's class at school. So. You understand the situation here? You understand that I could lose my licence over something like this?' Paul was starting to get very red in the face. 'Did you stop to think about that? Does it seem fair to you, does it seem right that I should lose my licence because you want to chat up schoolgirls?'

'But I –'

'Not that you got very far, probably. Wasn't it the first thing I told you? Under twenty-five? ID. No ID, no alcohol. It's the first thing you learn when you start working here.' He stopped and huffed deeply. 'I knew it was a mistake hiring you. A waste of time.'

'Should I – ?'

'No!'

'But –'

'No!' Paul slammed the drawer of the till, narrowly missing Danny's hovering fingers. 'No! No! No! Just get your things and just, just leave. Well, go on then!' The last words yelled as Danny backed away from the till wondering, just a little, what it would be like to take his former employer's head and smash it repeatedly against the shop counter until all the noise stopped coming out of its mouth.

'Hello?' Anka answered Peter's mobile and Alice was tempted to hang up but of course her name was now flashing on the display.

'Hi, Anka. It's Alice. Um, is Peter there?'

'Oh. Alice. Hi,' said Anka without enthusiasm and then, 'Bubbles! It's Alice.'

Bubbles? she thought. *Bubbles?* Wasn't that the name of Michael Jackson's chimpanzee?

There was a rustling and Peter came on the line.

'Peter! Congratulations! I had no idea . . . I mean, I didn't know you were on that page already.'

'Thanks, Alice. I guess it is kind of sudden but, you know, we just realized it was something we both really wanted and there didn't seem to be any reason to wait around so . . .'

'Yes. Well, congratulations.' She didn't seem to be able to think of anything else to say. *Congratulations*. There was a chewing noise. 'Peter, are you eating? I'm trying to have this big, emotional my-friend's-getting-married conversation and you're eating all over the moment. Besides, do you know how gross it is hearing someone chew when they're on the other end of the phone?'

He swallowed hastily. 'Anka made these amazing Polish snacks. *Rogaliki* – a sort of almond pastry. They're very good. Hey, remember how Tom used to come out of the bathroom talking on his phone with his flies undone? Do you think anyone ever noticed he was calling them from a toilet cubicle?'

'Ewww.' Alice sat down on the carpet. 'So. Details? When's the big day? Where will it be?'

He made a noise that was a telephone conversation's version of a shrug. 'We haven't quite decided yet. Maybe the registry office at the town hall.'

Did he sound irritated? Alice looked at her watch wondering whether it had been too late to call. In the past, of course, she would call Peter at any time, whenever, confident that he would be pleased to hear from her. She'd called him drunk from parties, bored from airport lounges, tired and emotional at the close of a horrendous deadline. It was odd, this new feeling of circumscription. She tapped her fingers. What were the rules about calling in the evening? Not after nine? After ten?

'Well, tell Anka congratulations,' she said finally. 'And sorry to call so late. I kept meaning to call and somehow it always seemed like a time when you'd be busy, and then I thought it was getting silly how long it had been so I just . . . called. Too late.'

'Of course it's not too – hold on a moment –' She could hear him talking to Anka but couldn't make out any words. He came back on the line. 'Sorry, what were we saying?'

'Just about to hang up,' said Alice with what she hoped sounded like gaiety. 'Just saying goodnight.'

She thought that there was just a hint, a glaze, of something in his voice that was pleased in the wrong way. Something in the voice that suggested she'd always been the one to turn him down and that now the boot was securely on the other foot and laced up tightly. By comparison, her own uncovered toes were small and weak and pink, vulnerable as newborn baby mice.

'Goodnight,' said Peter.

'Goodnight.'

Alice slumped back against the wall. Then she picked up her phone again and tried not to dial Martin's number; she certainly did not want to dial Martin's number; if she dialled Martin's number it would only make him believe something that wasn't at all what she meant. She dialled Martin's number. Then she felt ashamed and sort of regretted it when he answered on the third ring sounding pleased and eager. At the same time, though, she sort of didn't.

According to the history teacher Mr Spalding, 80 per cent of the genetic characteristics of most white Britons came from a few thousand Ice Age hunter-gatherers who'd followed wild horses and reindeer northwards and later been trapped when the rising sea turned their peninsula into an island. Staring around the school canteen, Emily was creeped out by the notion. It was like the film she'd seen on TV last night, with the hero waking up on the planet of a weird, inbred clone army. Picking at her salad, she regarded her schoolmates. Kara appeared older than she was because she was so tall, Anita was short and milky-looking, Laura was irredeemably freckled. Yet still she felt she could see a certain family resemblance around the cheekbones and, on the telephone at least, each had exactly the same voice.

'It was so brave of you. I never thought we'd get served,' said Anita.

'He was really weird though,' said Laura. 'Did you see how he looked at you, Kara? Ugh.'

'You know he got thrown out of my brother's year for stealing? Luke says he was always odd, never spoke to anyone. Luke says,' Kara lowered her voice so that they had to lean forwards to hear, 'he's the sort you can imagine *doing* something.'

'What do you mean, *doing something*?'

Kara looked at Laura impatiently. 'Like you hear about when those kids go crazy and kill their classmates. It's always the quiet ones . . .'

Emily forked a cube of cucumber. Give thanks for school salads. The sort of food Alice brought home was nausea-inducing. Just looking at it she could imagine the fat sliding down her throat, her blood pressure rising, her digestive system slowly clogging with white dough, oil pooling around her nose and in the cleft of her chin. She ate the cucumber.

'And in sixth form,' Kara continued, 'he always wore this old trilby and these trousers that looked like they'd come from a dead man's suit.'

Emily had been pleased, when she arrived at school, to find herself taken up by the prettiest girls in the class – she liked her friends to be aesthetically appealing – but by now she'd worked out the group dynamics and realized that she was a sidekick. She hated to be one of the sidekicks. She put down her plastic fork.

'He lives next door to me.'

They turned and stared at her.

'Yeah?'

'I see him all the time' – and then, just to annoy Kara – 'I actually think he's, you know, okay. When you actually know him like I do, I mean.'

Kara shrugged. 'Whatever. I'm just saying what Luke says.' She looked at Emily's plate and wrinkled her nose. 'Are you really going to eat that pasta?'

They were all silent for a moment. Kara and Emily stared at one another.

'Did you hear about Chrissie Adrian getting mugged behind the parade?' said Anita. 'Did you hear what he said to her? He said, "You're too ugly to rape." Can you imagine? That's just so, like, humiliating. I mean, on top of everything else.'

Laura shook her head. 'Is she okay? Is she at school? I think it's worse because it happened so close to home. You expect to be safe somewhere you've known all your life.'

'That's so not true,' said Kara, breaking her staring contest with Emily. 'Statistically you're most likely to be attacked by someone you know well, by a family friend or member. Somebody who lives next door.'

'I think she's quite pretty,' said Anita.

Emily sighed and pulled her tray forwards and addressed herself to the rest of the cucumber and tomato on her plate.

After school she changed into her shorts and T-shirt and did circuits in the back garden: squats, crunches, push-ups. Co-opting Alice and Janey's childhood toys she hula-hooped and skipped in the middle of the lawn. *Go for the burn.* Her body felt fat and sluggish – she thought regretfully of the gym pass hanging in her bedroom back home – but there was still plenty of time to pull into shape for the summer. She had a lot of bikinis.

At the end of the tenth circuit Emily stopped and drank some water. She could feel her legs prickling the way they did sometimes after strenuous exercise. While she waited for her breathing to come back under control she considered the rest of her body. She looked herself up and down with the clear eye of a booker at her old modelling agency. Her tan was distressingly faded but her calves felt good and taut. They felt *bouncy*. There was a clearly defined space between the tops of her thighs. Thighs that rubbed against one another were one of Emily's major life fears. She pulled up her T-shirt and pinched the skin on her stomach with one hand and then stretched: most of the flesh pulled away, meaning that it wasn't excess.

From a consideration of her genetic background, Emily felt that ultimately things could go either way weight-wise. Her father was thin and sinewy ('stringy', Carol said) but then his mother, Emily's grandmother, was an immense woman with swollen legs that transitioned directly from calf to foot without bothering to become ankles – so who knew? She lay down on her back, bent her knees and placed her hands by her ears with her fingers pointing towards her shoulders. After a moment she pushed her hips upwards until her body and head were off the ground and her arms at full stretch. She held it until the muscles began to really scream.

Until the summer when she was sent away to camp, Emily had considered her own mother, whatever her other faults, to be glamorous and pretty, with her red hair worn short at the back and sides and longer on top in a manner that exposed the full length of her neck. It was only after she'd returned from Camp Woodsmoke with head lice, a pocket calorie-counter and a wristful of grubby, braided friendship bracelets that she'd begun to notice Carol had gained a little weight. That she shouldn't wear such tight-fitting slacks in such bright colours and that neither should she expose so much of the browned, crêpe-paper skin where her necklaces hung down between her breasts. It was the same summer that she discovered her father wasn't coming back from the 'business trip' to Florida and that her mother was dating *call-me-Paul-I'm-not-trying-to-replace-your-daddy*. It was the summer also when her mother's laugh had begun to sound like fingernails on a blackboard – something that could most regularly be observed once the cocktail hour was well advanced.

Inspired by a disturbing vision of Carol in a favourite, too-small lime-green swimsuit, Emily completed four more circuits before going into the house to shower.

The baby was sleeping in his cot. Moving quietly and with the nervousness of someone not used to being alone with babies, Alice helped herself to a biscuit from the ceramic jar, a Fox's Party Ring. Mauve, yellow, sugared pink and frosted orange – shades that, when Alice was younger, had seemed to be the exact and authentic colours of happiness. She'd always chosen pink while Janey took the orange. Alice bit into the biscuit now and felt the sweet crunch of the hard icing. All the different colours tasted, of course, identical in reality. A few crumbs fell on to a newspaper left on the table from breakfast.

'I bought some for the Brownies,' said Sarah, pointing to the biscuits, 'and ended up with these ones spare.' Sarah led the local Brownie pack. She opened the fridge – 'Oh, the milk' – and went to fetch it from the front doorstep. Alice idly scanned the headlines of the newspaper. Across the world things were still being lost: money, banks, jobs, houses. A new and virulent strain of influenza had been recorded in South America. Alice thought, not for the first time, how she'd wrongly assumed that momentous historical change was finished in the Western world; that everything, ultimately, had become the same; that the future would simply be the present repeated.

'Is it church or registry office?' said Sarah, coming back into the kitchen. 'Or, you know, a stately home or something? I mean, is it religious?'

'Umm.' Alice, who hadn't spoken to Peter since the briefly awkward telephone conversation, tried to remember what had been said. 'Peter's not religious.'

'But didn't you say she's Polish? I thought most Poles were Roman Catholic?'

'So are Peter's family but he's *very* lapsed. I suppose he'd probably have a church wedding if that was what she wanted though.'

Several times she had meant to phone him again. She'd thought, *After dinner, after I shower, when I get back from the shops.* She'd promised herself that she'd go and visit them. He hadn't been in touch either. She leaned over and picked out a pale yellow Party Ring.

Sarah poured boiling water into the teapot. 'It's funny, I only met him once or twice, but you two always seemed to be hanging around together so I thought, before I knew about Callum this is, I guessed that you and Peter were going out. Isn't it funny?'

Alice nodded; it really was hilarious.

'Is she nice?'

'She's . . . fine.'

'Only fine?' Sarah looked at her curiously.

'No. I mean, good. She's good, great, fantastic. I guess I just don't really know her that well. She's quite young.'

The baby made a snuffling noise and they were both silent for a moment listening, but then he stopped. Sarah put the teapot on the table and sat down. Alice stared at the tabletop, at the grain of the wood, at all the tiny little lines and knots that seemed to float in the varnish.

'Alice? Hello? Alice, are you okay?' Sarah pushed a cup of tea across the wood towards her. 'Are they staying in London?'

'Who?'

'Peter. And his fiancée. Will they be staying in London after the wedding?'

'I guess.' She should go and visit them. Except that when she thought about such a visit her expression grew bright and guarded. She felt herself becoming polite and horribly *social*, and it made her a little depressed.

'You don't sound very happy.'

'Of course I'm happy. I'm delighted. Everybody loves a wedding.' She smiled and sipped the hot tea. The friendship needed some time to readjust, that was all. Things needed to be reassessed, new perimeters drawn up and new bases laid. But she still couldn't help feeling unfairly let down and unreasonably discarded. She still couldn't help feeling sad, which was ridiculous because everything was surely working out for the best.

Leaves had sprouted on the apple tree and the winter clattering of the branches had changed to a softer, almost watery shushing. As spring lengthened, fattened, the blossoms came out on the suburban cherry trees and drifts of pink and white flowers collected along the kerbs, browned slowly into rotting piles. A sparrow built a nest in the eaves outside of Alice's window, and she spent hours watching the birds dart in and out, in and out, in and out. Often, during that moment between wakefulness and sleep, she had a troubling sense of things being at once very small and then very large, set against a star-pricked backdrop. The thought, when it came, seemed almost physical.

Martin took her to the artificial lake where he had a fishing licence. It was a weekday and no one else was casting off from the banks. The still, brown surface glinted in the sunlight, and Alice threw a pebble far out into the middle of the water.

'Hey, you'll scare the fish away.' Martin looked up from fixing his bait on to the hook.

'Sorry. I thought I might see them, you know, jump or something,' said Alice, who had really thrown the pebble because suddenly the surface of the lake was too still, too perfect and glassy. She admired the ripples that ran back to her.

Another week they ate at a Harvester restaurant with its serve-yourself salad bar in the shape of a farmer's cart, and several times they went to see movies: one that Alice wanted to watch and that neither of them enjoyed, and one that Martin chose and was disappointed by though Alice, secretly, was rather entranced. Once at another restaurant they started to talk about Janey again, but Alice was relieved when Martin brought the conversation back around to himself.

'Sometimes I start to think about slipping out of life like that, and it seems . . . attractive. Just beginning over,' he said. 'Could I do it, do you think? I'm a failing estate agent with an ex-wife and a four-year-old daughter and sometimes I stop for a moment and it's like, *whoa, what just happened there?* Do you remember my band? Selling houses was always just a way to pay the bills until we got signed. It was only temporary.' He struggled to spear a tomato all slippery with coleslaw. 'I can't shake the feeling that everything I have now is still only temporary; it's as if I can't quite admit that potentially this is it.' Martin held the tomato down with one fingertip and got his fork into the flesh. He allowed himself a small smile of triumph. When he spoke again the words were directed less to Alice and more towards his plate. 'Girls and music – that's what it used to be. Girls and music.'

Mostly, though, Alice stayed in the house and found that the house, anyway, seemed to be changing around her, unfolding and opening like one of the little cardboard models she had collected as a child – flat shapes that folded and slotted together to make miniature three-dimensional buildings. Now, though, everything was happening in reverse. The walls peeled back and the roof lifted off. The paintwork flaked, the lawn lengthened, the concrete cracked.

On the telephone she tried to talk to Isabel. She wouldn't think about Peter.

'Are you okay?' said Isabel. 'We haven't spoken properly for ages. Why don't you come up to town more? You're only a train ride away.'

'Yes,' she said into the receiver. 'Mmmm. Oh really? No,' she said. She was bad at long-distance relationships; people became so inter-changeable in the abstract. Everyman was not a piece of the Continent. Rarely was the heart truly engaged. To give in to thoughts like that was a little like screaming as loudly as possible undercover of a fairground ride.

'I don't like to think of you stagnating all alone down there,' said Isabel. 'You're going to turn into some weird eccentric and forget how to have rational conversation.'

Tom continued to call. He had spoken to Peter, he said. They were concerned about her. The publisher was concerned about the book. *It was a wonderful opportunity. If Alice didn't feel able. Good money. Regretfully. Replacement.*

'Why don't you do it?' said Emily. 'Why are you so demotivated?'

'Okay,' said Alice. 'Okay. I'll go.' She blinked and blinked her eyes but they felt thick with tiredness, watery and red-rimmed.

Wearing the faded blue silk kimono that usually hung by her bed, she wandered out into the garden. The long grass of the lawn tickled her bare ankles. The blackbird, startled, began calling. *Hello, hello, hello.* It was past midday and warm with the promise of a long, hot summer. In the herbaceous border her father's lupins were already in flower, creamy petals threaded with pale pink. She leaned against the grey trunk of the apple tree, her head surrounded by rustling leaves, the rough bark biting into her back. It was the words that made her hesitate. She was no longer certain that they were anything more than an ingenious screen masquerading as something important and true. She no longer knew whether the consolations of self-expression or beauty were sufficient.

'Alice! Alice!'

She reached out, picked a leaf and began methodically shredding it, thinking, *And wasn't it only yesterday that I was sitting in this tree with Janey and there was so much of everything, so much future everywhere and it felt as though we could never use it up.* What would Janey have made of the past seventeen years? She was always there, Janey, somewhere in the past but nearby. She was always just outside the door waiting in the draughty porch, peering through the keyhole, tapping lightly, with one finger, against the wood.

'Alice! Alice!' Emily stuck her head out of the dining-room window and called again. 'Alice! Martin's here.'

She threw down the remains of the leaf, the ragged skeleton, and went inside. She'd decided to drive to visit Ericsson, and Martin was supposed to be helping her to buy a car. It was an indulgence and would eat up the small advance she'd been paid when she finally signed up to do the book, but she justified it to herself by thinking of the money she was saving on rent (she had offered to pay her parents something but they'd refused). Also, being in the suburbs without a car had begun to feel infantilizing in a way it didn't in the city where lots of perfectly reasonable adults failed to drive.

'Why don't you just get insured on your dad's car?' Martin had said the other day. 'Isn't it sitting there in the garage?'

'That car,' said Alice, 'is my father's pride and joy. I worry that I'd scratch the paintwork by looking at it or something.'

Now she paused in the hallway and ran a hand through her hair. It felt greasy.

He was leaning against the door frame cleaning his nails with the edge of his credit card.

'Alice,' he said, staring at her. 'Is everything . . . okay?'

Alice looked down at herself. The dirty kimono. The bare muddy feet. 'Ah, yes,' she said, lighting her cigarette. The heavy drone emanating from her laptop that was the latest album by an experimental doom-metal group from Seattle. It sounded, Alice conceded, as though she might be about to slaughter a goat. A chicken at least. 'Um, won't you come in? I need to shower quickly.'

In the living room Emily was sprawled on an armchair in front of the TV in a vest and a pair of baby-blue shorts. One bony-kneed leg was swung over the padded arm of the chair and the light streaming through the windows spun a gold band across her hair. On-screen an American politician was being interviewed. Emily sucked the tip of her thumb as she stared not at the picture but at the space it occupied in the slightly stuffy room, shifting her body sometimes in search of a more comfortable position. *Talks with China . . . the importance of China's friendship in these troubled economic times . . . now is not the time to discuss . . . environmental policies . . . human rights.*

They drove across the flyover and up by the old airport towards the second-hand car dealership owned by Martin's friend. There was a traffic jam; the faint choke of exhaust fumes, the silent drivers, close but quite apart, tapping on their steering wheels in time to private music. Set back on either side of the road were all the large out-of-town stores: for DIY, for food, for toys.

'That gallery you took me to?' said Martin, driving with one hand. 'I liked those paintings but I didn't really get the photography. I mean, anyone could have taken those pictures, right? I could have taken those pictures.' He laughed and shook his head.

She stretched and yawned. At night at the racetrack the sky was always sullenly overcast, emptily grey, and the wind whistled through the stadium. When, unable to sleep, she thought of the reddish track she sensed rather than saw black dogs behind her, snapping at her heels. And when she finally slept those same black dogs came streaming, one after the other, through her night dreams.

'What really gets me is how much they sell for. Crazy money.'

She watched his profile and imagined being married to it. It was a Saturday and they'd left the children at his parents' house while they ran weekend errands. Their car smelled a little of dog. A child's learn-to-read book lay discarded on the back seat. They wondered where to go on holiday next year. Alice imagined the sort of existence where you could book August a year in advance.

'Did you catch the news earlier?' he said. 'America and China? And that politician who's always talking about scrapping our nuclear programme. It's outrageous. Doesn't it mean something that apart from France we're the only country with a proper military presence in Europe, the only ones capable of actually making a difference in the world? Isn't there something to be proud of in that feeling of going abroad and knowing that there's this power behind you? Old-fashioned firepower like America has.'

Alice sighed. 'Obviously I totally disagree with everything you just said, but yes, I suppose I can see how that way of thinking could become addictive. That doesn't make it a good thing though.' She fiddled with the radio dial. Martin kept it tuned to some station that always seemed to be playing comfortable rock.

The car was a two-door dark blue Nissan. Already far cheaper, Martin's friend said, than it would have been even six months before. He was wearing, with a cheap grey suit, a Ford baseball cap, so that he looked a cross between a down-at-heel encyclopaedia salesman and a mechanic. At first, he said, it had been the new-car market that was hit: people who used to change their vehicle every couple of years deciding that what they'd thought of as a necessity was, in fact, a luxury. Now it had trickled down to his business. He looked around the forecourt gloomily, snorted, and went into his office leaving them to stare at the Nissan.

'It's a good car,' said Martin. 'And he's knocking a hundred off the price as a favour.' He prodded one of the front tyres with his foot. 'Trust me; this is a good car for you. I wouldn't let you buy it if it wasn't a proper deal.' He beamed.

Alice went inside to discuss the paperwork. The salesman unlocked a small safe behind his desk and took out a jewellery box and a small gun in order to reach a pile of papers underneath. Alice stared at the weapon. 'You have a gun?'

'A gun? No, no, I don't.'

'It's just there,' said Alice, pointing.

'Oh! Oh that. Yes, well, I only have one safe,' he said, putting the gun back inside. 'So I have to keep everything together. It's for protection. Now, how were you thinking of paying?'

'Gosh. I had no idea that it was so lawless out here. Commuter trouble?'

He shuffled the papers huffily. 'Sure, sure, so it seems fine at the moment, but you've been following the news? What we could very easily have on our hands is a survivalist, Mad Max-style situation.' He pulled down the bill of his baseball cap. 'When we're fighting over the last mouldering vegetables in the supermarket, the last clean water, the last can of petrol, that gun will be my passport.' He was starting to look rather red in the face. 'Everyone who's been laughing behind my back! You'll all see! Rat soup will seem pretty good by then – and don't think I'll be giving that out to just anybody.'

'No, no, of course not,' said Alice to placate him. 'I wouldn't dream of asking for your rat soup. I mean, I'm sure it's going to be lovely, but –' she looked up and was rather pleased to see Martin come in. 'Where do I sign?'

He hummed a little as he drove them back. She tapped on the dashboard. She was suddenly seeing the whole map of the Continent through fresh eyes – no longer a series of disconnected places but an undulating strip of asphalt. 'I am a citizen of Europe,' she said to Martin.

'*Oui*,' he said.

At the next set of traffic lights he turned and looked at her and smiled.

'What?' she said. 'What is it?'

'I was just thinking how good that car is for you. I'm pleased we were able to get it.'

Around them, the Tudorbethan houses all looked like perfect doll's homes. In the soft, late afternoon air the golf course curved gently over the brow of the hill. Lining the edges of the roads the cherry trees, each one now a mass of greenery, radiated goodness and well-being. She looked at him again and wondered if it would be possible to live like this, with much unsaid but with kindness.

'When do you go back to London?' he said. 'I'm afraid that when you go back to London you'll forget me.'

'I don't know,' said Alice, because suddenly it was not so very long until her parents returned. She should start looking for a flat, she supposed. She would be gone before the end of the summer, drifting back into the city. 'I don't know what I'm doing,' she said, and wound down the window on the passenger side so that the air rushing in blew through her hair and made her eyes water.

The Polynesian island of Henderson is one of the most inaccessible places in the world. Danny looked down at the book in his lap and realized that he'd read the same sentence three times. From where his deck-chair was positioned he could more interestingly see, at an angle across the lowish wooden fence, Emily sitting on the doorstep drinking a bottle of mineral water and painting her toenails from alternate pots of enamel, first pink, then silver. (It was warm for the time of year; everybody had been saying that.) He wanted to speak to her but to do so would break the carefully maintained illusion that the houses were separated by more than a thin adjoining wall; that they were, after all, detached.

Though lacking in natural resources the island was home to a tiny community that relied on supplies brought by trading canoes from other islands. He leaned forwards to get a clearer view, and even that small action caused Selkirk, slinking alongside the fence, to stop and growl until Danny sank back down to the familiar position perfected during the weeks since he'd been asked to leave the off-licence and alternative paid employment had continued to evade him. He heard his stepfather's car pull into the driveway, and turned the page. Compared to the thinness of his finger bones, the joints, he noted randomly, looked large and swollen as though he had arthritis. The car door slammed. They were back late from church; perhaps the sermon had gone on for longer than usual. He'd pleaded off with a headache, though really he was feeling guilty because during the week he'd broken a promise to his mother regarding his habit of casual shoplifting. (And, as ever, he'd told himself that it was most definitely 'the last time' but felt the futility of the gesture even as he formed the words.) He didn't care to go to church feeling like that.

When the trading canoes stopped arriving at Henderson, the islanders – who possessed no ocean-going vessels – found themselves cut off from the rest of the world. Leaning forwards again, Danny gave Emily a little wave and a flash of his rictus grin, but she didn't see him and got up and went inside. Selkirk snapped his teeth disdainfully and then followed. One day, Danny thought, he was going to lean casually over the fence and say something to her. *A hundred years later a Spanish ship, stopping to look for drinking water, recorded that the island was uninhabited.* From the kitchen, he could hear his mother finishing the Sunday lunch that she'd begun cooking before church: roast beef and potatoes and frozen peas, though it was more properly salad weather. He turned back to the book and read on until they called him inside.

'I was looking online and it's twenty-six degrees in Spain today,' she said as they sat down to eat. 'You're sure you don't mind being left alone when we go? There's probably still time to look for a flight.' She tucked her hair behind her ears and smiled. Danny made a non-committal sort of noise.

'The meat's a bit overcooked,' said his stepfather, jabbing his knife into the mustard pot. 'It's dry.' He transferred the mustard on to the edge of his plate. 'Did you see next door's guttering as we came in? She'll have a flood if it rains now – maybe I should say something. And have you seen the garden? Those weeds will spread.'

His mother nodded. 'I *have* noticed more weeds on our side recently. It's going to be tricky for Tom next spring if they get a good grip.'

'It's not on really.'

The sun was strong in the garden but inside the room, because of the angle of the house, the light was dim. The garden looked like a whole other world. The room, by contrast, was small and a little cluttered with pot plants and photographs and the china elephants that his mother collected. On the sideboard, in a silver frame, was a photograph of his great-grandfather who had been killed in the war. They shared a family resemblance, he and the dead man, especially around the brow-bone.

'Maybe you should have a word about the guttering. She's probably not used to looking after a house and garden.'

His stepfather nodded. 'What I really wonder is, what will Tom and Pam say about that dog?'

'Mmmm. I'm going to get the joint from Richardson's next time. Dawn at work was telling me that he gets lovely organic joints from some farm in Sussex. Now, do you know if it's safe to drink the water where we're going? We should check that, don't you think?'

Danny had the book open on his lap underneath the table. He turned the page. *Of the former inhabitants, all that was found were the remains of a series of stone shelters set up, in groups of two and three, with good views of the ocean.*

His stepfather, looking across, coughed meaningfully. Danny shrugged but then slipped the book underneath his chair and addressed himself to the steaming plate of food. He was glad his mother was happy, but was glad also that no one, viewing them side by side, would assume a blood relationship between himself and his bulky, sandy-haired stepfather. He wondered what Alice and Emily were having for lunch. Noodles or pasta or some such – he couldn't imagine Alice cooking roasts.

'If you stay here you'll have to keep an eye on next door as well,' said his mother. 'When they go down to the coast. It will be nice for Emma to see a bit of the country before she flies back.'

'It's *Emily*,' said Danny. It was immensely irritating the way his mother always acted as though she knew people that she didn't really.

His mind wandered.

Perhaps you'd care to join me for a drink?

But of course! she said, blushing. *I'm so glad you've finally asked me.*

Yes, it was clear that he had to speak to Emily. He clenched his left hand around his fork with new determination.

There'd been no one at the reception desk when Alice arrived at the Lighthouse, and now the old man with the watery eyes had trapped her in the corridor. 'I haven't had sex for twenty years,' he announced, looking her up and down. 'Can't imagine it, can you?'

Excited laughter came from around the corner. The man glanced over his shoulder, swore, and, leaning heavily on his Zimmer frame, manoeuvred himself with surprising speed into a nearby cupboard filled with cleaning products. 'Don't tell them where I went,' he hissed before closing the door, just as two eight-year-old girls dressed in brown culottes and yellow T-shirts careered into Alice's legs. One was wielding a hairbrush.

'Did you see the man?'

'The nice man with the walky frame?'

'We want to help the nice man.'

'I think he's in that little cupboard over there,' said Alice, crouching down and pointing. The Brownies squealed and began wrestling with the door as she continued towards the day room, a despairing *bugger it* floating after. On the way she sighted two more Brownies reading to an old woman who was trying to sleep, and another pushing a broom up and down the corridor underneath the water-colours and charcoal sketches. At the entrance to the day room she found Sarah.

'Alice! Are you here to see Mrs Austin? I've brought my Brownies to visit. I know it really cheers the old people up.'

Alice looked; the day room was swarming with brown-and-yellow girls. She couldn't see Mrs Austin anywhere.

'Mrs Austin said she thought you'd be coming today,' said Sarah.

'She's up in her room with a bit of a headache. Such a shame! We're going to sing campfire songs in a moment and she'll miss it all. I just need to round up some more audience . . .'

On her way to the first floor Alice passed Sandra surrounded by a silent group of girls. 'And in just ninety minutes – that's the length of a football game for any of you who are still a little too dumb to grasp the concept of time – in just ninety minutes all that's left of you is a tiny, tiny pile of dust . . .'

She knocked on Mrs Austin's door.

'Don't come in! I'm ill. It's almost certainly contagious.'

'It's me, Alice.'

'Are you alone?'

'Yes.'

'Good. Quickly then. Close the door behind you.'

Mrs Austin was sitting in a chair by the window reading the *Telegraph*.

'It amazes me how few of these banking men have shot themselves,' she said, folding the paper. 'I suppose it's not in fashion any more. So when are you off to the coast?'

'Next week, I think. I should know definitely by tomorrow.'

'Do you have a map? I have my set of Ordnance Surveys at home. You'd be welcome to borrow one. Let me see . . . I think you want OS 124. Here' – Mrs Austin reached into her bag and took out a small pocket knife – 'take this. You never know when you'll need a pocket knife.'

'Er, thanks.' Alice put the knife into the back pocket of her jeans, hoping it didn't count as an illegal weapon. 'You must tell me if there's anything I can bring next time I visit.'

'As a matter of fact I'm rather hopeful that I won't be here when you return. The doctor says I might be able to go home in a few more days; it's such a relief. If one thought one was doing something useful in this place then one might endure, but as it is . . .' She stopped. 'What was that? Did you hear someone knocking? Hello?'

The door swung open and a pale-faced woman in a floral house-coat came into the room. 'The music's playing again,' she said loudly. 'Like I was telling you the other day, Margery, when I was trying to remember the name of the tune.'

Mrs Austin's nostrils flared slightly, but all she said was, 'Perhaps once my visitor has left –' There was a high-pitched whistling noise. 'Your aid, Elizabeth.' Mrs Austin raised her voice and gestured to the woman's ear. Elizabeth nodded, smiled and reached up to fiddle with the fawn-coloured box.

'It's a hymn,' she said, almost shouting. 'It's definitely a hymn of some sort. The tune is so familiar – if only you could hear it. I can almost make out the words.' She opened her mouth wider and a sound came out that was nothing like music.

'Almost entirely deaf,' Mrs Austin whispered to Alice. 'I can never understand what it is she's trying to sing.'

Elizabeth turned away and Alice got up to close the door as two more Brownies appeared in the corridor.

'Brown Owl said that Mrs Austin isn't feeling well so we've come to read her a story,' said the smaller one.

Alice smiled at them. 'That's very kind of you, but I think she'll be okay. She's just going to have a little sleep . . .' She realized that the Brownie had put her foot in the way of the door. 'Honestly, Mrs Austin just wants to go to sleep now.'

The larger one whispered something and the smaller one nodded. She looked up at Alice. 'We've been talking to the nurse. We want to know, do cats get cremated?'

'I think they can be.' Alice jiggled the door handle; Mrs Austin was feigning unconsciousness.

Tears started in the larger Brownie's eyes and her bottom lip began to tremble.

'Also,' the smaller one continued, 'we want to know if cats can become ghosts?'

'Uh . . . would you like a biscuit?' Alice picked up a packet of chocolate digestives and held them out hopefully. 'Take two. In fact, take the whole packet.'

'I'm going to get Smudge cremated,' said the smaller Brownie, extracting a biscuit. 'Smudge is badly behaved. Yesterday he did his business in Daddy's slippers and then he scratched me. After he's cremated I want to get a nicer cat. A kitten.'

She moved her foot and Alice took the chance to pull the door closed, waving goodbye and muttering something about telling Brown Owl how helpful they'd been. She sat back down.

'Sorry about the biscuits.' And then after a while, 'Do you believe in ghosts, Mrs Austin?'

'I used to enjoy a ghost story around the campfire – and at Christmas, of course, it's traditional – but actual ghosts? I don't think so, dear. Now the Indians in Canada, I remember my brother writing to me once, have ghost stallions and bears and spirits and all sorts of rather jolly-sounding mumbo-jumbo that can't possibly be believed in. Haunted ground that you aren't sup-posed to walk across and so forth. Do you remember what I would tell you girls at camp when you'd scared yourselves with ghost stories? I used to tell you all to think of a bicycle. Just think of the logic of a pair of wheels. Think of spokes and brakes and gears. "How," I'd say, "can a ghost exist in the same world as something as rational as a bicycle?"'

Alice nodded.

'Yes,' continued Mrs Austin, 'a bicycle really does give a marvel-lous sense of perspective on things, I've always found.'

Mme Collette was late for the French lesson but then it was the last day of term and everything was late, everything slow. Teachers and pupils drifted through the motions of the school day, but secretly everyone knew that already it was the holidays and everyone was thinking of the next day, and the next. A chain of empty, unscheduled days stretching ahead like glass beads strung on a necklace.

Emily was brushing her hair, thinking, *This is the last time I'll sit in Mme Colette's classroom; this is the last time I'll lean back on this chair in just this way; this is the last time I'll write on the back cover of this blue exercise book.* All summer term she had been excavating a hole in the bottom of her blazer pocket, picking away at the stitching, and now, just before the French class began, an exploratory finger finally worked its way through the bottom seam.

Mme Colette hurried in clutching a pile of papers. '*Bonjour, bonjour, ça va?*' The class struggled to their feet. '*Wee, sa-va bee-anne, mercy, Madame, et vouz?*' Mme Collete put down the papers and mopped her forehead with a tissue. '*Oui, oui, ça va. Asseyez-vous.*' They opened their textbooks. Emily was pleased to see that the French family they'd been following – Mama and Papa and the two kids – were finally leaving La Rochelle where they'd been malingering for an entire term and were going *en vacances*. She rummaged in her bag for the new vitamin supplements she'd ordered online and dry-swallowed two. Mme Colette droned away in front of the whiteboard. She always stood with her feet too wide apart as if the classroom were the deck of a ship and she were constantly bracing herself against the roll of the waves.

Emily began filing her nails, thinking of her own *vacances*. A family trip to Hawaii had been suggested, but though she would have liked to have gone surfing and hung out in a bikini, she couldn't get past the thought of Larry lying by the side of the pool, of her mother laughing hectically over cocktails with little umbrellas. Her father had invited her to stay, but he had a tendency to act as though she'd stopped growing up the day he left home and was forever just turning thirteen, and anyway, ugh, Florida had been dull the last time she visited. 'I want to stay for the summer vacation,' she'd said, and Carol had agreed. A desire to go home and all the good things that suggested tugged against the idea of staying on with Alice, who tended to let her get on with things and who was, generally, a lot more restful to be around than either of her parents. *En vacances* Pierre wanted to go swimming. His sister, Sandrine, wanted to play tennis. Emily suspected that Alice spent a lot of time thinking about her missing sister – more, at least, than she ever admitted to. There was a good section about bereavement in chapter eight of *Choose to be Happy*; you had to go through certain stages – denial, anger, sadness – and it seemed likely that Alice had some sort of emotional blockage, only it was difficult to talk to her about it all. She was a bit repressed. Perhaps during the holidays it would be possible to explain the stages of bereavement without mentioning the actual book; Alice was bizarrely prejudiced against *Choose to be Happy*.

It was warm in the classroom; one of the windows had been opened and sounds from the playing field drifted faintly among the desks. Kara was slumped in the next seat, her cheek resting on her hand so that the skin was all pushed up. Emily could just *watch* the wrinkles forming. She wriggled the tip of her finger back into the hole in the blazer pocket. Through the window she could see, in the distance, the office blocks in the centre of town gleaming green and silver in the afternoon sun, and off to the right a huge crane, burnished red, dominated the heat and the stillness. The black hands of the clock on the classroom wall ticked slowly towards the half-hour. The French family went out for seafood and then the last bell rang (the last bell!) and the classroom erupted with noise and movement. Emily, eschewing the end-of-term festivities, grabbed her school bag and ran down the staircase oblivious to the calls of the hall monitor and a white-coated teacher from the science lab (she was leaving!). Through the heavy swing doors at the front of the school (illegally using the staff and visitors entrance!), pulling off her tie (no more uniform!), she came on to the driveway and ran towards the gate, rushing through the shadow cast by the Scots pine that grew just inside the school wall, and out into the sidewalk and into the road.

Tyres squealed on the Tarmac, but she didn't see the Audi until after Danny had caught her arm and pulled her back. She made a noise like *ouffff* and sagged a little as the driver braked and then roared away. Her legs were trembling.

Eventually she began to register that Danny was talking at her, still holding on to her arm, 'Emily? Emily. Are you okay?'

She nodded, feeling that she wanted to sink down on to the kerb and put her head between her knees.

He stared angrily where the car had gone. And then, rushing, 'I thought you might like to come for a drink? With me?'

She opened and shut her mouth a few times but couldn't seem to begin to speak. Looking up, she saw Mr Spalding hurrying towards them.

'Daniel? What are you doing here? Emily? What's going on?'

Danny dropped her arm and stepped back.

'Hmmm?'

Out of the corner of her eye she saw Danny disappearing into the crowd of schoolchildren who had suddenly spilled out of the pupils' gate. She straightened her blazer. The last thing she wanted was to have to go back into school.

'I'm fine. I guess I'm just going now, Mr Spalding.' She turned away, hurried and then slowed down once she'd rounded the corner and was out of sight of the school. She'd half expected him to be waiting for her there, but the street was empty. *Oh Lordy*, she thought with her mother's voice as the sounds of her classmates rose up around her like chattering starlings, like little blue and grey wavelets breaking against a concrete shore. Emily did some deep breathing and then she got out her compact mirror and rubbed pink gloss over her lips. She reapplied concealer to the blemish on her chin, the mirror shaking a little in her hand, and brushed back her hair. Soon she began to feel considerably better. There was a tap on her arm.

'Shall I carry your bag?' Danny said. 'I can walk you home.'

When Alice was alone in the house it seemed to regain a feeling from her childhood of an expanding space, filled with mysteries, which turned the reddish bricks into a castle, a mansion house, a Gothic palace. There was the attic reached by a ladder, the cool larder in the kitchen, the dark space underneath the stairs where you could look at the wooden boards and see two strange, inky red marks that appeared to be either skulls or crowns depending on the way you felt, but that more prosaically were probably something to do with the lumber yard the planks had come from. From her bedroom window, through a gap between the facing houses, she could see the golf course where players moved across the fairway. She held her arm out straight in front of her and squinted along the line to her fingertips. *Pschw. Pschw.* Everything in the suburb – house, field, shop, tree – was really a stand-in for some other, more ideal thing, and this made it seem both beautiful and sad everywhere she turned and looked. She held her arm out in front of her again and tracked, silently, another unwary golfer. In the sunlight the small figure hesitated for a moment and then set out, shouldering a bag of clubs over the exposed sweep of the fairway towards the sixth hole.

Part Four

'Many a "tenderfoot" has got lost in the veld or forest, and has never been seen again, through not having learned a little scouting, or what is called "eye for a country", when young.'

How Girls Can Help to Build Up the Empire: The Handbook for Girl Guides
(1912)

Emily was sitting at the kitchen table studying the Ordnance Survey map and trying to feed Selkirk a digestive biscuit. 'What's the address again?'

'I wrote it down . . .' Alice waved her hand vaguely. 'In the black notebook.' She paused at the sink where she was filling water bottles and looked across into the garden because she had a sudden feeling that Janey was out there, sitting in the branches of the apple tree, fingering the ripening fruits. In Alice's head, Janey lived mainly in the summer, in one of those high, hot childhood days that come to define the season for ever, that become a sort of ur-summer of the mind. The doorbell rang, and underneath the table Selkirk growled softly when Emily got up to answer it, coming back into the kitchen with Danny trailing behind her.

'I found a copy of that film,' he was saying. 'The one with the girl who really looks like you.' He held out a small parcel, but Emily, who'd bent down to fuss with Selkirk, didn't notice. Alice smiled sympathetically. Since Emily's school had broken up for the summer, Danny had begun showing up occasionally on their doorstep, waiting awkwardly in the porch with his hands in his pockets. 'It's nice that there's someone your own age so close by,' Alice had said to her cousin, and though Emily looked unconvinced she seemed to enjoy bossing Danny around whenever he appeared. Alice turned off the tap and tried to be encouraging. 'All alone next door then?'

'Yeah.' Danny pulled at his fringe. 'They're back next week.' He looked down at the map spread out on the table. 'Hey, I know this place. My grandmother lives along the coast here.' He gestured to a small collection of houses. 'It's pretty.' Then he stopped abruptly as though embarrassed to have said so much, and put the package down on the table and stared at it.

Yawning, Alice pointed to where Ericsson lived. 'I've not driven there before so if you know a good route . . .'

'What do you think?' Emily showed Danny two bikinis. 'Green or topaz?'

He blushed and muttered something.

'The topaz looks good with my hair.'

Alice put the water bottles into a bag. 'I'm just going to see whether that washing is dry.' She had no idea what to expect in terms of hospitality at Ericsson's so she was packing lavishly – or rather she was throwing as many things as possible into the back of the car and hoping for the best. Emily had written out a list but then Alice had put it in her pocket, washed her jeans and reduced it to a hard wad of compacted paper stained with ink. She'd not yet confessed.

Danny stared at his feet. 'I didn't realize you were going today . . . I should leave you to get on with the packing . . .' and then to Emily, 'The film's for you to keep. I don't need it back.' He pushed it across the table towards her.

'I think green,' said Emily. 'Topaz can be sort of draining.'

He nodded. 'Um, I'm actually going down to visit my grandmother soon. Maybe we could meet up? Go to the beach or something?'

'Sure. Text me.' She glanced at Alice. 'It's probably going to be pretty dull down there.'

Alice pretended not to hear her. She was finding it an excellent strategy for living with Emily.

Driving out through the ends of the suburbs they passed the closed Woolworths store, the closed sandwich shop. A hopeful plastic sheet of advertising hung from a partially completed apartment block by the library; rooms sketched out as empty spaces in the air.

The building site was quiet in the late morning haze of another fine, beautiful day. Alice was tired with sore eyelids and a slight tension in her head. Even behind the wheel of the car she couldn't seem to shake the drifty, dreamy feeling. She'd been wrong to think work, action, would combat the enveloping spaciness.

She turned at the traffic lights and passed one final row of 1920s semis, their outer walls pebble-dashed to disguise the cheap brickwork beneath. If you travelled directly from Trafalgar Square along the old London road this was where you ended up, out where the first fields lapped against the edges of the London sprawl. Janey might have left this way. Janey might have followed the same road that they were taking now down towards the coast. Janey might have found a girl-sized gap in the universe and walked through it and completely disappeared. To the right three ponies stood switching their tails, welcoming visitors to Surrey, to pleasant towns and green villages still heavy with the wealth that flowed down from the City.

'It's too hot,' said Emily. 'I think I feel sick. Why are all the roads so twisted here?' she stuck her fingertips out of the window to feel the breeze across them. 'How long would it take for us to drive across the country?'

'Which way? From the bottom of Cornwall to the top of Scotland, say, would take around fourteen hours straight.'

'Right,' said Emily, 'fourteen hours. Yup.' She nodded as though this confirmed something, sank down further into her seat and then let out a howl. 'I forgot my phone charger! We have to go back.' Excited by the noise, Selkirk barked loudly, causing Alice to swing towards the verge.

'Don't *do* that! And I'm not going back just to get your phone charger.'

Emily scowled and closed her eyes. After a while she spoke again. 'Are you and Martin dating?'

'No.'

'Okay, but you sort of are. What will you do when you go back to London? Will you still see him?'

'I don't know. I guess I'll cross that bridge when I come to it,' said Alice. 'I'm not going to think about crossing it yet. In fact, I'm not even going to see the bridge for a good long while.'

Emily sighed. 'How does anyone ever know when they find "the one"?' She drummed her fingers on her leg. 'I mean, I just don't want to *settle*, you know . . .?'

They were in the Weald now, an area stretching over parts of Sussex, Surrey and Kent and once covered by the immense forest that the Saxons called *Andredsweald* – the place with no dwelling. A crowd of motorbikes roared past, figures in black leather who reached the crest of the hill ahead of them, each rider hanging suspended for a moment before disappearing out of sight. Emily fell into a doze but woke just before they crossed the windswept expanse of Ashdown Forest where the trees, cut down to fuel sixteenth-century ironworks, had been supplanted by yellow-flowering gorse. Shallow soil lay over sandstone rocks.

'So tell me about this artist again.'

'What do you want to know?'

'Just, you know, about her life and stuff. Not an art lecture.'

'Okay, so she was born in 1949 in the Lofoten Islands, off the coast of Norway, and moved to London during the 1960s. For a while she was a life model at the Slade art school, had an affair with one of the tutors and ended up going back the next year as a student. She painted a couple of fantastically influential pictures – *The Abbess* and *Herreninsel* – and moved to California to teach at CalArts. She was part of the Fem Arts programme, which was really –'

'Did she get married or anything?'

'Yes, she married this performance artist called Frankie K –'

'Dumb name.'

'– divorced him a year later, moved to New York, was a founding member of the Columbus Club and then moved back to London in 1989. Her patronage of the YBAs is considered to have been an important factor in their early success.'

Emily frowned. 'Kara says that feminists are basically women who've realized that men don't want to sleep with them, but I honestly think that's just a really stupid thing to say. I mean, obviously I'm not a feminist –'

'Obviously.'

'– but I do really appreciate everything your generation did for us.'

Alice raised her eyebrows. '*My* generation?' It was hard to know with Emily whether the fault lay with her grasp of modern history or her apparent belief that after twenty-one everyone was the same age and virtually dead.

'I just don't know whether a career is compatible with marriage.'

'Emily,' said Alice.

'Yeah?'

'Do you still feel sick? Try looking at something far away.' She changed gear and accelerated.

On the far side of Ashdown Forest they stopped to eat sandwiches in an airless tearoom with blue gingham tablecloths. Alice ordered a scone with a little pot of cream and a shallow dish of strawberry jam. Emily drank a bottle of mineral water and swallowed a small pink pill, two large white ones and a tiny yellow hay-fever tablet.

'I didn't know you got hay fever,' said Alice.

'I don't,' said Emily, putting the packs back into her aqua-blue tote bag. 'But I could. I mean, this is the countryside.'

Alice spread butter across one of her scones. The lunchtime rush was over and, except for a man by the window wearing a pair of sunglasses, they were the only customers left in the tearooms. Emily went outside to give Selkirk some water. The waitress, clearing the next table, glanced at her and then turned to Alice, directing her thumb back outside. 'That great big thing your dog? Shouldn't he be tied up then?'

'We don't usually. He's very well behaved.'

'I'm sure he is, but it's just that, well, the customers don't know that. I'm not sure it's such a good idea, the dog being loose. There're kiddies and old folk coming by all the time.' She picked up her tray. 'If it's all the same I'd be happier if you'd slip a bit of rope on him now.'

The man in the sunglasses leaned forwards. 'Local?'

Alice shook her head.

'Thought so.' He smiled. 'Don't worry about her. She just likes to think she's in charge of everything. Staying nearby then?' He was pulling something out of his bag.

'No. We're headed to the coast.'

'Well, still, take one of these in case you do happen to be passing sometime of an evening.' He handed her a pale yellow leaflet.

'Guardian angel gatherings?'

'That's right. We hold them on our farm – down the lane, just past the war memorial – all welcome. Have you found your guardian angel yet? No? Someone close to you passed maybe?'

'Yes. No. I –'

He rummaged again through the rucksack at his feet and took out a small white candle. 'Here, take this. You look as though you might have some use for it. I don't mean to offend, but the candle might help. It represents your angel.' He nodded and rocked back on his seat. 'It's not a Christian thing. I wouldn't call it *religious* as such. It's more spiritual. We have a sunset vigil around the fire and light our candles and talk to our guardian angels; you'll find that it's an incredibly powerful experience. Who is it that you're missing? A parent? A sibling?'

He reminded her of some of the psychics and spiritualists her parents had consulted after Janey left. *He smells need*, she thought, *damage*. She put her candle down on the table. 'No, thank you.'

The man sighed. Getting up he leaned over and stuffed one of the yellow leaflets into her bag. 'They all act like this at first,' he said to no one in particular, and then, to Alice, 'Tell them my name on the gate – John – and you'll get in at half price.'

He walked to the door, passing Emily on her way inside, and then paused and turned round to look back at Alice. 'Be safe now. Be strong. Remember: our emotions are the only truth we have. You owe it to yourself.' He waved and disappeared.

'Who was *that*? He looked as though there was something breeding in his hair.' Emily picked up the white candle from the table and frowned. 'Don't tell me there's not going to be electricity at this place.'

They drove on towards the coast, to where the Downs began to gather themselves and there was a sense of expectancy in the landscape. Along the tree-shaded roads the sunlight flashed repeatedly on, off, on, off. Alice looked at the map and judged they were almost at Karin Ericsson's house. Looming above were electricity pylons like Wellsian Martian fighting-machines, and above them the silver-bellied planes. Underneath everything, though, there was a constancy to the patterning of the South-East; a medieval system of villages, farms and fields that had remained essentially unchanged, unchanging. *It's so crowded everywhere*, thought Alice. There was a thickness to the landscape: Bronze Age burial mound, Iron Age camp, Roman villa, Saxon church and parish. Every surface seemed to have been covered with correcting fluid and then written over, the process repeated and repeated until the white paint was scratched and flaking here and there so that layers of older text showed through in indelible dark blue ink.

She blinked against the tiredness and tapped her fingers on the steering wheel. Had Ericsson really stopped working? She imagined walking into the house and finding piles of paintings completely unknown, unseen, unexamined. Surely that would be something worth writing about?

'Are we almost there?' said Emily.

'I think so. Can you look at the map? I think the turning must be around here somewhere.'

'There!' Emily pointed to a rutted track leading off to the right up ahead. 'That must be it.'

They turned and soon the track brought them to a small, single-storey wooden house. Inside the car the metal buckles on the safety belts burned to the touch and the quiet July heat clung to their bodies, made their armpits damp and seamy. They climbed out and smelled warm earth and sweet clover. The walls of the house were painted a faded blue, but the paint had blistered so the grey wood beneath showed through in strips and patches. Moss grew over the low roof. A rusty mesh fence strung between wooden posts enclosed a small front garden, bramble-ridden, nettle-strewn. Tall swathes of pinkish rosebay willowherb manifested through the trees.

'This is the place then,' said Alice. 'I mean, as far as I can tell this is the place.'

'This is a dollhouse,' said Emily.

Alice thought it looked like a fairy-tale cottage. Inside they would find seven dwarves, or a wicked witch, or a sleeping princess. It was so still, quiet except for the bird calls – goldfinch, blackbird, swift – that punctured the air, the little flashes of brown and black and blue that darted among the leaves of the hawthorn and oak trees that crowded over the tin roof. Alice and Emily slumped against the bonnet of the car, reluctant suddenly to go through the gate. Selkirk padded off into the undergrowth and they heard him rustling awhile and then nothing.

'It looks kind of derelict. Maybe she's moved? Should we knock or something?' Emily said. 'It's weird that she doesn't have a phone.'

Alice nodded. Ragged net curtains obscured the view through

the two square windows. They pushed open the gate – it was a child-sized gate that came to just below Alice's waist – and rapped on the door and the sound in the silence was like an insult.

The ticket inspector put him off the train and the man in the ticket office escorted him out of the station. He was going nowhere, they said, without the money to pay for a ticket. Shouldering his rucksack he walked along an oak- and birch-lined riverside path headed south, and as he walked he turned over in his mind again the way that the car had skimmed past so miraculously close and how it had wrought a sort of connection between them.

The day of the car, when it was hot and everything had felt at once dry and sticky, he had carried home her school bag and she'd invited him inside the house for a glass of water. Nervous, he knew that he hadn't spoken as much as he should have, but she talked a lot so that was all right really. There had been a first long awkward silence in the kitchen and he'd almost put his glass down and walked out, but then she'd got on to the subject of school and it turned out that one of the idiots from his sixth form was the older brother of one of her best friends, except – it seemed complicated – she didn't really like the girl that much. They had forged some sort of conversation over a mutual disparagement of the older sibling. Shared dislike, Danny was learning, greased the runners of friendship far more effectively than any joint appreciation. Since then they'd *hung out* several times; it had been almost easy. And it was a relief to be with someone who didn't know how unpopular, how friendless, he'd been as a child.

The river gleamed fatly, silver-brown water deepening into pools of green underneath the willow trees that clung to the bank. After a while he paused to drink from the hip flask he carried, and the water tasted metallic. He hitched up his trousers (he'd lost more weight; the waistband flopped around his hips) and pulled down the brim of his trilby to shade his eyes, though it was dimmer here underneath the trees, the strong July sunlight hitting the path in patches. Of course she might be surprised at first to see him, but he'd felt strongly, after spending a day alone in the house, pacing a little in the garden, that it would be wrong to let her go back to America without trying to explain more clearly how he felt and about the connection between them. A small voice suggested that his mother, had she not been in Spain, would have questioned this course of action, and that Emily, when he found her, might also see things differently, but he was determined not to be dissuaded. The more he replayed their last conversation in the kitchen, the more certain he was that she'd pretty much invited him to visit (*Sure! Text me!*). They had a beach date. Also, it was summer and he was alone and bored and this was, after all, something like an adventure.

He was walking now on a narrow strip of path, a reluctant public right of way between the river and the backs of houses, grand in the Edwardian Gothic style. Green lawns stretched down towards the water. Despite the fine weather the gardens were uniformly empty, the windows and doors of the houses closed. Everything was shimmering slightly in the heat. Hungry, he gently patted his empty stomach then picked a stalk of grass to chew on, wondering whether he could get down on his hands and knees and graze like a sheep, a cow, a small snuffling bunny. The grass was sweet.

Round a corner the footpath swung abruptly away from the water to run along the side of a high, ivy-draped wall. Drifting through and across the brickwork, the sound of music and voices could be heard. Danny pulled himself up into the branches of a low-reaching oak until he could see over to where another wide lawn swept down towards the river and where tables and chairs had been set up by a little jetty. A row of stone urns held bright red geraniums. Smartly dressed men and women stood around in small groups with waiters moving between them bearing trays of drinks and canapés. The French doors at the back of the house were open, and a man dressed in a dinner jacket appeared between them and called something – Danny couldn't hear from where he sat in the tree, but he guessed it was a summons for food or some other entertainment because the guests immediately began moving towards the house, stepping one after another through the doors into the darkened space beyond. Several of the women had left hats and handbags on their seats at the tables on the jetty. A single cigarette smouldered in an ashtray.

Danny twisted round to look back down the path, but there was no one else walking there. There was no one in sight on either side of the wall. A sign affixed to the brickwork warned that there were guard dogs loose, but not now presumably, not with all the guests. His stomach groaned. He threw his rucksack under some brambles, stretched forwards, grasped the top of the wall with both hands and swung on to it, balancing and then dropping down to the lawn.

In another moment he was at the jetty and had snatched up one of the handbags – dark brown leather, a glint of gold – before 'Hey there! Stop!' and a middle-aged man in a pale grey suit and with a glass of champagne in his hand was running down the lawn towards him. Danny stood for a long moment holding the bag, stupidly watching the man running, gaining the centre of the lawn but then suddenly slowing, the man's free arm swimming up to clutch at his chest and his mouth opening. *Help. Heart. Help.*

The French doors at the top of the lawn stayed closed and dark as the man began to sink slowly to his knees. The champagne flute fell but made no sound as it bounced and rolled across the grass. Danny moved a step forwards only to stop and turn, still holding the bag, and run instead for the river, jumping into the water and splashing round to the other side of the wall, stubbing his toes on the muddy bottom. He pulled himself up on to the bank and listened for voices, but there was only silence and the squelching of his plimsolls. He was shaking. He picked up his rucksack, pushed back his wet fringe and began to run fast through the trees.

The black leather chair by the window, occupied by an untidy bundle of papers, was by Mies van der Rohe: the Barcelona chair. The organically modernist dining table looked, Alice noted, like vintage Aalto. Placed in its centre a group of white candles, like church votives, had dripped wax on to the varnished surface, which Karin Ericsson now picked at with her fingernail, frowning and creasing further her heavily lined face. Despite the heat she wore an ankle-length denim skirt and a pale, long-sleeved blouse, and on her feet were heavy black boots. The outfit gave her the look of an Amish or Mennonite woman.

Alice and Emily sat awkwardly on what appeared to be an eighteenth-century chaise longue covered in grubby pink sateen. 'I have a print of yours at home,' said Alice. Ericsson winced slightly, as if the sound of their voices hurt her. So far she had remained silent. Alice tried again. 'Do you have any work here? Do you have a studio? I'd love to see it.' The woman put a finger to her lips, shaking her head.

The expensive furniture looked quite wrong inside the thin-walled wooden house that creaked as you moved about. It looked like real furniture within a cardboard stage set. The house was a garden shed. The house, if you got down and huffed and puffed, would blow right away. Emily tipped her glass backwards and forwards, suspicious of the water, which had a brownish tinge. Ericsson lifted her own glass and drank deeply, gestured with her hand for Emily and Alice to do the same. Alice's glass sweated in her hand, cool against her fingertips, and despite its colour, the water didn't taste particularly unusual. Emily put her own glass down without drinking and licked her drying lips.

Ericsson continued to stare at them in silence. The skin that was visible, on her wrists and hands, her neck and face, was burned deeply brown and she smelled, though not unpleasantly, unwashed. Then she stood up – she was tall, too tall for the dimensions of the house – and beckoned to them and turned and crossed the room in three paces. In the hallway she opened doors quickly on to a room with twin beds, a bathroom and a galley kitchen. At the end of the kitchen another door opened on to a small garden carved out from the surrounding trees, where a tin bucket waited next to a water pump. She turned and gestured back towards the bedroom, and when she spoke her voice was deep. 'You must excuse me but I have only this one spare room for the two of you. And where is the dog? Tom said you would be bringing a dog?'

'He ran off when we stopped the car. I should go and look for him,' said Alice.

'He'll be okay,' said Emily, flopping on to one of the beds. It was true: Selkirk was the very definition of self-sufficiency.

'Good. So now I'll leave you to relax from the journey.' Ericsson nodded sharply, turned and closed the door behind her.

Alice sat down on the other bed and felt the springs give.

'Did you see that skin?' said Emily, shaking her head. 'She seriously needs to start moisturizing.'

Alice lay back and her eyes flickered and then closed. The room smelled a little damp and unused. It smelled a little of the gas that fuelled the immersion heater. A sour smell. After a while she heard Emily stretching out on the creaking bedsprings. She heard a dog barking somewhere outside and the noise followed her, at a distance, far into her afternoon dreams.

After he had stopped running he walked for a long time through the fields away from the river to dry his clothes in the afternoon sun. His shirt, the one patterned with little pictures of Mexican horses, smelled faintly, muddily, of the brownish, greenish water. He looked inside the handbag and found a wallet with three damp twenty-pound notes, some pound coins and some loose change. The bag he buried down a rabbit hole. If he could walk calmly outside in the sunlight it would prove to everyone that he was a man with nothing to hide. *Help, heart.*

At the train station he bought a ticket for the next southbound service. It seemed the most natural thing to keep moving south, away from the house and towards the ports, the sea, the edge of the country. He feared, and didn't care if the fear was irrational, that already the police were looking up his details on some computer and that if he went home now he'd find his mother's semi surrounded by uniformed men and women. Standing nervously on the platform he imagined the man in the pale grey suit lying alone on the lawn. He imagined figures in white moving towards him across the bright green.

On the train, still thinking about the police, he hid in one of the toilet cubicles, looked at his face in the scratched mirror for signs of a killer. There was a stupid pale band of skin around his forehead where the trilby, now forgotten underneath the oak tree, had rested. His stubbled jaw had a guilty look – he hadn't shaved for several days – and he took a disposable razor from the pack in his rucksack and released a gooby dribble of sad, industrial pink soap from the dispenser. In the small fluorescent cell Danny scraped hair from his jaw and imagined being reborn from among the grey and blue plastic and chemical smells of the toilet cubicle on the South-Coast Express. On the way to the station he'd taken a pair of scissors from a small chemist's shop and now, in a gesture towards disguise, he hacked off the long hair that fell over his face, the deflated, defeated quiff. He would slough off his old self as one might remove congealed grease adhering to the grating of an extractor fan. There was very little to hold him to his old form. The short and long hairs collected in the aluminium sink basin. If only he could carry on removing layers until his skin was pink and tender and he was clean and fresh and innocent as a baby.

'This is it?' he said to his reflection. He had always assumed that he'd been saved from the water for some higher purpose. He had flattered himself that he was to do something good. True, his life so far had been formless and disparate, but until today his crimes had been petty, his infringements against his fellow men had been slight. Now he began to wonder. He looked down at his hands, which were very white and trembling slightly in the fluorescent light, looked up again and met his own eyes, and wasn't there something there, some shadow he'd never noticed before? How stupid to assume he knew who'd kept him safe underneath the surface of the water that was so cold it burned exactly like flame.

When Alice woke her body felt sweaty and her mouth uncomfortably dry as if all the moisture that should have been inside had seeped out on to the surface of her skin. She blotted her armpits with a handful of tissues. A metal bowl filled with more of the brownish water had been left on the floor in the middle of the room, and she lifted it awkwardly and drank and then set in down and splashed water over her face, leaving it to run down her neck and darken the collar of her green-and-white-striped sundress. Emily's bed was empty. Alice took her mobile out of her canvas bag thinking that Isabel would enjoy hearing about Karin Ericsson, but there was no signal. After pulling a brush through her hair she tied it up in a ponytail to let what air there was cool the back of her neck.

What an incredible place. At the foot of her bed was a 1962 Diane Arbus print. None of the works she'd seen hanging on the walls, she suddenly realized, were reproductions. In the front room alone she'd noted a Richter and a Sherman. Alice touched the wall next to the Arbus and it felt a little clammy. Irreplaceable paintings and photographs left completely unprotected in a house with no security system, a house so flimsy it felt as though you could cut through its sides with a bread knife. Fragile canvases exposed to damp and to the smoke and heat from the white candles strewn throughout the house. Hours of people's work, the fabric of lives, squirrelled away where no one would ever see them. The eyes of the woman in the Arbus print were a little mad and staring.

In the kitchen something was cooking on the hob. She inched

her way past banks of tin cans – filled on the right, empty on the left – and opened the back door. Emily was sitting in an old striped deckchair repainting her toenails. The greyish wooden garden table was set for dinner. Unlit white candles, tall wine glasses, heavy silver cutlery, a basket of bread. There was deep-red wine in a decanter and a carafe of brownish water. Ericsson came to the back door wearing an apron. 'Please,' she said, gesturing with her hands, 'please sit.'

'Can I help? Can I do something?'

'No, no, just please take a seat. I'll be bringing the food.' She disappeared back inside.

Alice nodded and moved over to the empty deckchair next to Emily. It was finally cooler now and very quiet except for somewhere in the longer grass at the edge of the garden, the sounds of crickets always just out of reach, always just out of sight. Selkirk lay panting by the water pump and Alice threw a stick towards him but he ignored her.

Ericsson came back outside carrying a silver terrine, which she set in the middle of the table before lighting the candles. She nodded and spread her hands. Alice lifted the heavy lid and Ericsson handed her a ladle with a beautifully ornate handle that bit into Alice's hand when she grasped it. Inside the terrine were what looked like baked beans with little pieces of sausage. She ladled some on to each plate. Before they began eating Ericsson bowed her head and clasped her hands as if to say grace, but her lips were still. Overhead the sun was finally disappearing. Emily forked up some of the beans, tasted them and raised her eyebrows at Alice. Alice took some for herself. They *were* baked beans. The sort that came in a can with processed sausage.

'You have some amazing work here,' said Alice, to make conversation. And then curiously, and because as a journalist she was used to walking into situations and asking intrusive questions, 'Aren't you worried about security?'

Ericsson shook her head. 'No one can think there's anything worth stealing in this tiny place. Look at it. Besides, they are always making more paintings.' She passed Emily the bread basket. 'Eat! Eat! I am glad to see you both eat. So, Alice Robinson, Tom tells me I should know of your work. You are a most well-regarded critic, he tells me. I have to say, you look younger than I expected. How old are you?'

'Thirty-four.'

'Hmmm. Not so *very* young. I apologize. My English friends always told me I am too direct. So. You have not written about me?'

'Only a very little. I wish it had been more, but of course the Tate published their monograph six years ago and it seemed so complete. I never felt that I had anything to add, no new narrative to bring out . . .'

Ericsson snorted. 'You should worry less about "new". So a scientist seeks the unknown and makes discoveries, good, but except for a very few, a handful of people, making art is always about dressing the old things up in different clothes.'

'But your great pieces – *The Abbess, Herreninsel* – surely *they* were something new?'

Ericsson laughed. 'I don't believe so. Besides, what I say is not necessarily a criticism, just an observation. Now then, tell me, Alice, aside from the lack of burglar alarms, what do you think of my little house? Is it not perfect? It is exactly the sort of place I was seeking: quiet and hidden and, perhaps, somewhere nice for the grandchildren to come and visit.'

'I didn't realize you had –'

'A child? Yes, a little-reported fact. She stayed with her father when I moved to California and now we rarely speak because, you know, I abandoned her. At least that is what I think I am supposed to understand from her silence. You will note, please, that when her father sent her to boarding school in order to pursue his own career then *that* was not abandonment. Anyway, she has two children and I have hopes that she will change her mind about us meeting.'

'Harsh,' muttered Emily, pushing her beans from side to side.

'Her latest idea is that I want a family only to gather information for my work. As if I was some robot or alien, some unfeeling thing that needed to live – how to say? – *vicariously* through another. Alice, have some more wine, do; it's very good.'

There was an awkward silence. Alice poured wine into their glasses as Emily surreptitiously scraped her beans and processed sausage on to the grass for Selkirk to eat. She set the decanter back in the middle of the table and tried to bring the subject round once more to Ericsson's work. 'It's so good to finally meet you. I wanted to tell you that I've been thinking a lot recently about your *Sakhalin* exhibition. It still seems incredibly relevant – even more relevant, you could argue, than when the work first appeared – and so far from being exhausted. Could you ever think of going back to it?'

The older woman shuddered and shook her head. 'Listen: as an artist I did well, I was considered "successful" – but why? Often success came because I was making great use of some horror that never belonged to me. With the *Sakhalin* work I said I wanted to give voice to the unvoiced, to draw attention to their struggle. Nonsense. I was preaching only to people, ineffective people, already converted to this cause or that. It was cheap sentiment. After almost fifty years I find, looking back, that the only thing apparent in my work is my own ingenuity. I pretended to be struggling with faith and doubt when really I was only making clever puzzles for children to unpack.'

She fell silent. Emily scuffed at the earth underneath the table with her toes. As they'd been speaking it had grown dark in the garden.

'When I was a little girl in Lofoten,' said Ericsson, 'we would go out at night in the late autumn and look for the *nordlys*, the aurora borealis. We would climb the hill behind our village and lie down and wave our handkerchiefs at the green lights sweeping across the sky. It was so beautiful. To watch them felt like flying on our backs in the cold grass. We thought they were responding to us. And then, of course, we would become scared and run home to our mothers and hide our faces in their skirts as they sat knitting or reading by the stove. We never told what we had been doing.'

She stood a little stiffly and picked up the terrine.

'You've both had enough? Good. Tomorrow I have some business to complete in town and must leave you to yourselves. I will be late returning – probably you will be asleep – but the day after that I shall be entirely at your disposal. Perhaps we will try to make something better of it all for you then.'

She turned and went inside. Emily walked off to look for something in the car. Alice rolled a cigarette and sat a while smoking, and presently she could see the woman as a dark shape moving across the window at the back of the house, lighting a series of candles that flared up like small, bright flowers growing behind the polished glass.

The south coast was littered with structures of defence. There were military canals, offshore bars of granite, concrete sea walls, wooden groynes, eerie curlicues of barbed wire strung along the clifftops. There were things designed to keep people out, people in, land from falling, sea from encroaching, beaches from shifting position. Danny sat cross-legged on top of a concrete pillbox watching the landscape. Yesterday, chancing upon the bunker, he'd thought that he might sleep somewhere down inside, but the earth floor was marshy, strewn with litter and smelling faintly of urine, so instead he'd spent the night dozing uncomfortably out in the open with his back to one of the walls, waking continually to stare wide-eyed into the countryside dark.

He ate the second ham sandwich that he'd bought at the railway station and watched a chestnut-coloured cow amble gently across the next field. Further away a flock of sheep grazed on the dewy grass. If he couldn't go home then he might as well, in part for lack of any other plan, continue down the coast towards where Emily was staying, though from now on he'd walk, keeping out of sight among the fields and hedgerows. It was unfortunate that already his cheap plimsolls had cracked widthways along the sole and that without his trilby the sun bore down painfully on his head at midday. He felt distinctly at odds with the world once again. Shut out. Locked out. The happiness of yesterday morning, the hopeful walk along the river, already seemed immeasurably far away. More than ever now he felt as though he were treading water underneath a sheet of glass.

The sunlight glinted on the St Christopher just visible where the

Mexican shirt was opened at the neck, and his thoughts continued to bat against the man in the pale grey suit. He clasped his white hands in front of him and they appeared ugly, like monsters bred in darkness. What sort of fiend was he? As he looked up, the blueness of the sky seemed to dissolve into thousands of tiny flickering spots around the blacknesses of the telephone wires; those looming wooden poles planted by the side of the road and all at once ancient and modern and shading from grey to brown to rusty orange.

Last night because of the heat they'd left the window open when they fell asleep. With a wind springing up, Alice had been awakened by the rhythmical rattling of the single glass pane. Outside, the trees had sounded first like the ocean and then like hoof beats, and Selkirk had begun to bark until a sudden fierce gust blew the window shut with a loud bang that left her staring wide-eyed in the darkness, the last line of a dream running through her head: *I want, I want, I want to go home*. Janey had used to say that, Alice thought, as a little child she used to say that and it upset everyone because, of course, she was always already home.

Karin Ericsson had left by the time they got up in the morning; the key was on the table in the front room with a note that simply said, *Enjoy!* In the afternoon Emily rubbed factor twenty on to her browning arms and legs and refused to move from the plaid rug. She'd taken one of her new pills and they seemed to be making her drowsy. From the bushes Selkirk watched them blankly. Alice, finishing the red wine from the night before, picked up the blister-pack. 'Do these really work? Can I try one?' She popped two out of the foil, hesitated and then added a third, washed them down with the wine and lay back. 'What are they supposed to do?'

Emily turned over on to her stomach. Alice watched the clouds scudding overhead and smoked a cigarette and then she sat up again. 'Do you want to see if there's a way down to the beach?'

'No. I want to *relax*. I want a tan so I don't look like a freak when I go home. I heard that all the water round here is sewage.'

'I think I'll take a walk then,' said Alice, and got up. The sun was hot and she was tingling all over with something, some feeling. She thought a walk might help.

'Hey, do you think she'd mind if I borrowed some of those white candles later? They'd be good for meditation exercises.'

'Uh huh – but just the ones that have already been lit. And don't move them all around.'

Emily nodded and closed her eyes.

'I might go down the coast, go into town, so don't wait for me when you want to eat later. Will you be okay here?'

Emily flapped a hand at her.

At the edge of the garden Alice chose a path at random, moving from the hot brightness into the cooler, dappled air underneath the trees, smelling the acrid scent of fox piss. The forest there was mainly oak and beech, the undergrowth a mass of green brambles studded with tiny white flowers. Hidden birds called out from high up in the canopy. The earth was dark and rich with grey oval pebbles that looked like prehistoric eggs, and clumps of ghostly wood anemones. She walked without purpose and with a head still hazy from the pills and the wine, and after a while it became difficult to judge distance, impossible to reckon how far she'd come. With no buildings, no views outside of the trees, there was a timelessness to the wood. It could have been yesterday or tomorrow as plausibly as today. She looked down at herself and wouldn't have been surprised to see that she was ten years old again, twelve, sixteen.

There was an immense old oak tree, its centre hollow – a heart rot. Inside was a damp cavern filled with dead leaves and flat, reddish-brown ox-tongue fungus. Outside the tree continued to throw out new branches and green leaves. She ran a hand over the thick, grey, elephant-hide bark, crumpled and folded over itself like a piece of rough fabric draped over the wire frame of a dressmaker's dummy. A squirrel started away and ran up the side of the oak and out along a branch. (A body, she was thinking, couldn't lie undiscovered for long in these woods, in the heavily populated South-East of a small, heavily populated country. But then if no one was to look . . . If a body lay behind a rock, encased in brambles, stolen away part by part by small animals, smaller insects . . .)

She carried on walking, surrounded on all sides by bright green nettles. Sunlight filtering through the canopy turned the leaves of the beech trees into delicate, yellowish clouds clustered around the dark silhouettes of branches, and the smooth silvery trunks with undertones of olive and salmon were streaked with dark green lichen. There was a pond, the opaque water – it hadn't rained for weeks – sunk low in the ground so that a metre of raw, churned mud ran up towards the nettles that grew thickly around the edges. A wren hopped on to a tree stump intent on something, some business, entirely unconnected to her.

Eventually she looked at her watch thinking she should go back but realizing that she no longer knew which way to walk. She continued following the path she was on – there was comfort in following a path because paths are made by people and have a purpose; eventually the path would deliver her somewhere – and found herself climbing uphill until she was back at the pond; she was walking in circles. It was very quiet for a moment and a lazy bubble popped slowly on the surface of the water. (Janey lost somewhere beneath the water, blonde hair wrapping around the reeds, white fingers leached of colour floating upwards towards the oily surface.) She shivered. The trees seemed oppressive now, the gaps between them full of places for *things* to hide, and she was suddenly aware of how much she didn't want to be in the woods at night-time. The sea, she thought, lay downhill, away from the path. The undergrowth in that direction was filled with brambles but didn't look impenetrable. It would be best, perhaps, to find the coastline and then work along from there back towards the house. She picked up a large dead branch – earwigs scuttled away – and using it like a cudgel to beat down the worst of the plants, she stepped off the path.

Thin, stinging scratches soon covered her legs, but after some time she began to think she could smell salt and sensed a lightening of the air, and then, all at once, the trees gave way and she was standing on a clifftop edged with gorse, spiky green stems studded with little yellow flowers and filled with the buzz and drone of the summer bees. All of yesterday she had thought about swimming, about slaking off the heat in the cool salted water. She wanted to shake a growing feeling of watching the landscape without inhabiting it. She looked down to where the green slimed boulders on the beach cast long shadows, each one the size of a girl. Up on the cliff-top the trees crowded behind her, and to her right and left the gorse grew thickly to the edges of the land, stopping her from walking along the clifftop except by going back among the trees, but now that she was briefly out of the wood she was reluctant – especially with evening approaching – to return to it. She thought, also, that from the little pebble beach at the foot of the cliffs she might be able to walk around to the open Downs and come back to the house that way, along the road. Late afternoon sunlight sparked on the water, which was brown closer to the shore, becoming green and then blue as it stretched towards the horizon.

The cliff was not sheer but rather sloped, at first at least, at an almost generous angle. Here and there gorse bushes clung to the pale brown earth that topped the chalk that formed the main body of the rock. Alice lowered herself cautiously over the edge and began scrambling down, using hands and feet, keeping as much of her body in contact with the surface as she could. She moved quickly, not letting herself think too much, following the paths of rockslides that had carved little gullies into the side of the cliff face. Around three-quarters of the way down to the beach, when she was beginning to sense that she had almost made it, she faltered and stepped too heavily on a loose section of rock. A football-sized lump of chalk fell away from beneath her and she groped blindly with her hands as it loomed up, that great golden presentiment of loneliness, an opening vision, suddenly, of *I was not*. She tumbled down into it. She tumbled down into *I was not* and her hands opened and shut on fistfuls of air.

Emily, dozing on the rug, came to so abruptly that she guessed some noise must have woken her, but though she strained her ears, everything was silent. Even the birds were drowsy, it seemed, in the late afternoon heat. She sat up and reapplied her sun lotion though it was well beyond the hottest point of the day and the rays were gentler now. The oak and hawthorn trees cast long shadows that crept towards the little wooden house. Her mother had always said that Emily was cold-blooded, like a lizard, the way she lay out on a hot day basking for hours on end.

She picked up the book she'd been trying to read earlier, but it was one of Alice's: dull and slow. She dropped it on to the grass and contemplated her nails. Her hands and feet were perfect: the varnish wasn't chipped and the cuticles were neat. She drummed pink fingertips on a browning knee. Emily didn't find herself good company. Alice told her that she lacked inner resources, making that sound like some sort of moral failing.

She got up and went to look inside the house for her cousin. The rooms were empty, silent, and she found that now she was by herself she didn't really care for all the pictures Ericsson had hung about the walls. Perhaps it was just that there were too many or that they were too large for such a small space, but the canvases and prints seemed to crowd in on her, to watch her, almost, as she walked past. They creeped her out. She retreated back to the garden and called for Selkirk, but there was no response. She wished now that she'd asked Alice to come back for dinner; if her cousin had gone into town she might be away for hours, might not come back until very late. It had been some time since Emily had been so very much by herself. She didn't even know where the next house was, though she suspected it was not close. She yawned and walked back to the plaid rug and lay down, letting the last of the sun lull her back in to an uneasy sleep.

Alice was stood on a deposit of pale brown earth, a large, compacted mound of soil brought down from the top of the cliffs during a storm. She was elevated a little from the beach, but still the crumbling surface of the rock offered no good handholds and still the cliff ran almost sheer for a metre or so above her head. She scrabbled uselessly against the rock and pieces of England broke off, smeared her palms, stuck beneath her fingernails. From below, the cliffs already looked much higher and her attempt to climb down seemed the more foolish. She sat defeated with her back against the rock.

Tidemarks, a scum of dried seaweed, showed that when the tide was fully in it rose short of where she was sitting – at least in summertime it did. She was safe from drowning but caught at the edge of the island between the brown and white cliffs and the wilderness of the sea. Looking around the small pebble beach she shivered; the sun was dropping now, going, almost gone, and unlike a winter evening which falls swiftly, catches you unawares, this summer ending of the day had an added sadness to it that came from seeing so clearly the slowly dying light. No footpath led to the beach; there was no way up the cliff face; there would be no help until Emily alerted someone and a search party was sent out. She looked at her watch but the second hand was still, the mechanism broken, presumably, during her fall. She could see no other beaches along the coast in either direction; just the bone-white cliffs sliding in and out of the sea and, far away towards the east, the bluish-lavender towers of the power station at Dungeness, floating as if on some cloudy archipelago, like

Laputa, like the complex in Dubai which, when the money was found to complete it, would appear to hover on a cloud 300 metres above the earthbound city.

In the cooling air her green-striped sundress felt thinner and she put on the cardigan from her rucksack. A low ray of sun reflected a golden portal far out in the water and the sea began to take on a glaze of silver. It would soon be late enough for Emily to become concerned. Even now, most likely, she was calling Selkirk, walking down the road, stopping a car to ask directions to the nearest telephone box. Alice watched the small dark shape of a huge ocean trawler balancing on the horizon. What was beyond that grey rectangle? It could have been anything. She knew, of course, that it was France, but she couldn't *see* that it was France. Sitting now on the beach the idea that it was France was as much an article of faith as the belief that Janey was out there somewhere and alive. As much an article of faith as the belief that Emily would bring help. As much an article of faith, probably, as the belief that a woman alone on an island was still a woman.

There was a greyness enveloping the beach but so gradually it felt as though it was her eyes and not the daylight that was failing. Vision was stealing softly away. She began to consider, for the first time, that she might have to spend the night by the sea. During her confused ramblings through the woods she had lost all sense of where the beach was, of how isolated or how close to civilization it might be. There could have been a whole city just around the headland or a motorway on top of the cliffs just beyond the first screen of trees. Taking Mrs Austin's penknife from the rucksack, she walked up and down the beach looking for driftwood and found the remains of a dead tree, with its useless roots still attached, lodged between two large boulders, and she broke off branches and dragged them back up to the top of the mound where she would be safe from the tide. She arranged the longest, straightest branches diagonally against the cliff to form a sort of lean-to. The shelter wouldn't help much if it rained or grew stormy, but she hoped it might act as a windbreak. It was comforting in any case to be doing something.

Gulls circled overhead barking and screaming, yapping and whimpering. A thought came to her that just now she was as lost to everyone as Janey was, that perhaps Janey and all of the missing whose faces appeared on posters, in advertisements in the backs of magazines, were living on some hidden beach, some secret island. Strange white islands had appeared on the maps of the early cartographers, she remembered reading somewhere. Spirit islands that seemed to move, to dematerialize and transmute. Islands that, baffled ships' captains reported, were *no longer there* – though later mapmakers, accounting for these travelling landmasses, suggested that they had, in fact, been only cloud formations sunk low on the horizon.

When the stars came out they were beautiful and bright. She thought of Peter searching uselessly for the asterisms and constellations.

She built up a fire, laying smaller sticks in a pyramid formation surrounded on three sides by larger branches, and coaxed first thin white smoke and then finally a roaring flame. She ate an apple and smoked a cigarette and fed the fire. Once, when it was dying down, she crouched with her cheek almost against the hearth and blew on the embers until the flames came back and her eyes watered from the smoke. The light of the fire in the darkness made her feel at once more safe and more vulnerable. There was a story, she remembered, of a smuggler's vessel foundering off the coast somewhere nearby during a spring storm. The customs and excise men, when they arrived on the beach where the ship's cargo of brandy had been washed up, were at first unable to distinguish between the dead and the drunken bodies that lined the shore, the drowned smugglers and the intoxicated villagers strewn about between the boulders and, like those boulders, forming little deeper darknesses against the paler darkness of the beach.

The fire guttered in a sudden breeze.

'Janey?' Alice said into the darkness. 'Janey, are you here?'

In the early hours of the morning Danny neared the house. He walked nervously through the high rolling darkness of the Downs, and from every side of the path there came the slitherings and rustlings of small, unseen things. He found that his teeth were chattering and that the moon was a thin, unsympathetic crescent, high and silvery. At one point a car approached from behind and he shrank into the ditch out of sight of its sweeping headlights and it cost an immense effort to get upright again. The world made him lonely and repelled him, and he took this as a sign that what he had done to the man in the grey suit had made him finally unredeemable. *Oh, Emily!*

Unable to see far ahead Danny walked up and down the same stretch of road several times before finding the beginning of the track leading to the artist's house. He stopped and tried to check the time on his mobile, but the battery had died. In a few more hours he reckoned it would be light, but already there was, he saw it now, a strange cast to the sky beyond, a blushing luminescence that looked not quite like dawn. Wondering, he turned down the track. The hot days had baked the mud into hard ruts, huge troughs and deep furrows, and it was immediately much more difficult to walk. Around a bend the low, rectangular body of the house loomed up out of the trees and then he stopped, open-mouthed. Long orange tongues of fire blew out from the front windows, unfurled in the night air like expensive silk curtains. Pale white sparks dropped on to the grass below. The noise, though, was what kept him transfixed, the roaring, rushing, infernal sound of it. 'Emily,' he said, and he was shaking.

Looking around he expected to see people gathering, figures moving, but apart from the flames there was only silence. Keeping close to the trees he ran to the other side of the house where it was still cool and dim. From somewhere inside a dog was barking. The windows at the rear of the building were dark, and when he pulled open the back door there was heat but he couldn't see any flames. He made his way through a sort of galley kitchen into a tiny square hallway that was filling rapidly with smoke. One door opened on to an empty washroom but the other three were closed: two felt warm when he tested them with the back of his hand. The dog, wherever it was, had fallen silent. He pushed open the third door, stepped through and slammed it closed just as the fire broke into the hallway.

Smoke filled the room, drifting up to the ceiling, and Danny crouched down, bent at the waist like a man in prayer but coughing, half blinded, listening to the roar of the fire, feeling the polypropylene carpet squares, which made the tips of his fingers itch. He crawled towards the window, reached up and rattled the handle, but it seemed to be locked or jammed. A panicked mouthful of air filled his lungs with hot metal, bending him over in pain, forcing him back on to his knees. Already it was becoming hotter. 'No,' said Danny, scrabbling against the twisted fibres of the beige carpet. It came out like a pathetic baby's whine – *nooooooo* – and then his terrified fingers caught hold of a warm arm, a fistful of human hair.

She'd noticed a small stream, almost a run-off, that came trickling down the cliff, and she filled her canteen and sipped cautiously. It tasted like the water from Karin Ericsson's pump. As the sun heated up the rocks she lay eating a melting chocolate bar from her rucksack feeling comfortable and drowsy.

The cliffs marched away east and west, and it was pleasing to see the shape of the country, the curve of the landmass, spread out like a model, like the synthetic topography of a miniature railway set. Birds spiralled overhead: skylarks, swifts, gulls. A plane cut through the blue, travelling away from the island and leaving a white trail behind it like some exotic plumage of its own. She imagined Emily on the plane, Janey, Martin, Peter and Isabel. She imagined her mother and father, everyone she knew flying away and leaving her on the beach surrounded by the constant, not-quite-rhythmical sound of the sea breaking and the waves now and then slapping loudly at the green bearded rocks.

The sea looked calm in the light of a new day, and she thought now that if she swam out beyond the promontories at either end of the beach she might be able to see another bay with an easier path up the cliffs. Yesterday her head had been muddled by the pills and wine, she thought, but now she saw the ridiculousness of being trapped on this small beach at the edge of this island. Things like that didn't happen on the English south coast. It wasn't rational. It would make a good story – how she'd scared herself into spending the night on a beach. Peter and Isabel would laugh. But where was Emily? Hadn't she gone for help? Hadn't Ericsson returned?

She took off the green-striped dress and her plimsolls and piled them next to her rucksack, then picked her way over the pebbles to the edge of the water where little frothy wavelets ran up to meet her. The sea was cold but it was hard to walk on the rocky bed so she ducked quickly underneath to get past that first shock and, surfacing, sent up glittering handfuls of water droplets, hit the flat, briny surface with the palm of her hand to hear the sound it made. To the west the white cliffs gleamed bravely outwards.

She stroked away into the deeper water, where the colour, viewed from above, changed from brown to green, but still she couldn't see around the headlands. Already her blue rucksack on the beach looked small and insignificant. She didn't trust herself to swim much further out, but she went a few more arm's lengths, the waves seeming bigger now, more bodied, and then at last she was clear of the promontories, breathing heavily, scanning right and left. There was nothing. Only the cliffs, hard and inaccessible, dipping in and out of the sea. She could pick a side of the beach, west or east, and swim along the coastline, because there must be another bay somewhere, an access point, but she wasn't a strong swimmer and the thought of the sea fathoms beneath her made her shiver despite her warmed and aching limbs. Disappointed, she gathered herself to swim in, but, after pushing for some time through the water, realized that the distance between her body and the beach refused to narrow – that she was caught in some sort of current.

Alice turned and began to swim parallel to the beach, trying to ignore the rising panic and the rising tightness in her chest, adrenalin now battling with exhaustion. The cliffs were white, the sea was grey, the sky was blue. Everything taken from the same neutral, neutered palette, as the world might look when all the vegetation and all the living things had died. She seemed to be making progress, but then a sudden larger wave caught her from behind, tossed her head over heels, sent burning salt water up her nose. When she surfaced, she saw the rocks at the bottom of the cliff rushing towards her too quickly and tried to brace herself against the contact of flesh on rock. Bone on bone. She reached out with her arms but couldn't grasp the first rock and was slammed into it instead, then dragged back and slammed a second time. On the third rotation she had a moment to think that there wouldn't be a fourth chance and then her hands were clutching the rock, and then her feet were bracing against it. She was hauling herself up on to the jagged boulder.

She clung there weakly for a moment before pulling her feet upwards out of the sucking of the waves. In the distance, along the line of the cliff, was the beach and the small blue rucksack, bright and man-made against the pebbles. Fixing her eyes on the bag to help keep balance, she began slowly picking towards the beach across the rocks that crowded around the bottom of the cliff. Once or twice she almost slipped back into the grasping water, but each time righted herself with a pounding heart. And then she was limping over sun-warmed pebbles, unminding of how they bit into her feet, welcoming the stinging cuts on her legs and arms because they meant that she was alive. What, compared to the next breath of air, was of any real importance? According to Linnaeus, life began on an island, she remembered. Ararat was not a mountain but a body of land surrounded by the ocean. She bent over, her stomach cramping with salt water. And before Ararat, the first people escaping wet and scared on to higher ground at the beginning of the flood. Children's toys: cheerfully painted wooden boats filled with smiling camels and elephants and sheep to distract from the waterlogged bodies floating through the seaweed, their hands white and wrinkled, a little pink-tinged foam gathering in the upper air passages.

Danny sat in the hospital holding a cooling cup of coffee from the vending machine. He remembered the door of the room falling in and the dog bursting through ahead of the flames and hurling itself at the window. Fresh air had come pouring in past the broken glass and he'd somehow managed to drag Emily across the floor and push her outside. He remembered kneeling by the trees as the fire engines came racing up the track and then the firemen shouting and the heavy boots going back into the house and emerging with a second, limp body – the artist, he'd now been told, Karin Ericsson. The firemen had been preparing to go back inside a second time when the fire burst suddenly through the roof of the house and they all fell back.

Now it was several hours since Emily had been taken away down one of the long corridors, and as he waited his mind ran backwards and forwards between the burning house and the quiet, antiseptic room where she was, presumably, lying. His ankle ached from when he'd landed heavily going through the window. At first he'd tried to ask where Alice was, but after being endlessly referred, deferred and generally ignored he'd given up and accepted his slumped position on the plastic chairs. He was at once exhausted and agitated, profoundly tired but awake in a way that felt like the buzz of caffeine but wasn't. The receptionist stared at him and he smiled, but she looked quickly away at her computer screen. He straightened the blackened collar of the Mexican shirt and ran a hand through the space where his hair should have been. Every time he closed his eyes he heard footsteps and imagined a looming policeman holding out a dark-brown leather handbag. The bag was dirty from having been stuffed down a rabbit hole and it was smeared, of course, with his own incriminating fingerprints.

Seen through the high windows of the hospital the early morning sky was welcoming, and to pass the time he limped outside to look for Selkirk. The dog was tied to the hospital railings and lying down in apparent resignation, though the rope around his thick neck was worried and bespittled and in one place almost bitten through. Danny approached cautiously. It seemed wrong that the animal had saved his life and now, by way of reward, was tied up like a criminal. 'Would you like to go for a walk, boy? Time for walkies?' Nervously he fumbled with the knot. 'Good boy. Down, boy. Good boy.' Selkirk watched lethargically until the rope finally came free of the railings, upon which he suddenly sprang to life and jumped away barking and snarling, jerking the end of the rope from Danny's hands. The boy and the dog stood facing one another for a beat or two, while Selkirk continued to growl and flash his teeth. Heart thudding, Danny began backing away. 'Okay,' he said, holding up his hands. 'Okay, do what you like. I'm not going to tie you up again. I'm not your owner.' He backed away some more and then turned and hobbled towards the road. When he paused and looked behind he saw that Selkirk was following, trailing the remains of the rope.

Favouring his right ankle, Danny turned down one of the neat, bungalowed side streets with the front gardens done out in squares of pebbles and strips of concrete – low-maintenance gardens for the elderly residents. It was still early in the day and no one seemed to be about. Selkirk padded along beside him, companionable all at once. A net curtain twitched as they passed. Chez Nous and Casa Mia and Llamedos. He came to a small parade of shops with an Internet café that, despite the hour, was already open for business, and so he ducked through the doorway. Selkirk wouldn't let him near the rope but seemed content to wait outside on the pavement, panting slightly in the shade of the awning. Already it was hot again.

Except for the boy behind the counter the place was empty. The air was warm and dry, and the constant low-level humming of the machines was calming. He sat by the window and began scrolling through the news sites, looking for any mention of a death, an intruder, a thief at a party. *Help, heart, a pale grey suit on a bright green lawn.* He tapped his leg nervously. And then there it was: a small news item on the home page of a local newspaper:

Robbery: local businessman suffers heart attack.

Danny's hand strayed unconsciously to his St Christopher and then up to his mouth as he read on.

. . . taken to hospital where staff say his condition is stable. He is expected to make a full recovery. The suspect is described as a white male, approximately twenty years old, of slim build.

He let out a long sigh and was suddenly weak. He felt as though the ice had just cracked and that his vision had gone from a monotone, underwater murkiness to something fresh and colour-filled. The man was alive. In a daze he stood and limped out of the café and down the street that led to the beach. The horizon was all at once wide and open with opportunities. Selkirk paced alongside.

An old man was sitting in a deckchair by one of the breakwaters, a pair of binoculars resting on his lap, and he raised his hand to hail Danny over. 'Take a look through these, will you, son? I can't see so well sometimes but I'm on lookout duty, on watch.'

Danny took the binoculars and held them up to his face. They were old and heavy and he needed two hands to keep them steady. 'What am I supposed to be looking for?'

'Ships! What else? See anything?'

'No . . . wait, yes, there's a little . . . a yacht?'

'Make out its name, can you?'

'*Blythe Spirit*.' He handed back the binoculars.

'*Blythe Spirit*. That's good, that's fine. That's Mike Palmer's boat, that is. Thanks, son.' He began polishing the lenses. 'Two thousand years we've been on these beaches. The castle at Pevensey Bay down the road, that was a Roman fort once, then a Norman keep, and then in the war they put all the big gun emplacements there. I remember . . .'

Danny sneezed and the old man looked at him with concern. 'Feeling all right then, are you? It's just that you sneezed, see. Not got a temperature?'

Danny shook his head.

'Been near any foreigners? It's all over the Continent.'

'What is?'

'The flu! The influenza. They've got it over there and if we don't watch out we'll have it over here. That's why I'm out on the beach – been here every day since the pandemic was announced on the telly. Can't jump across water, can it, but they'll come in their boats.' He shook a finger in Danny's face. 'They come over. They travel down to France and then they come over here in their little boats to use our health service. I've got six grandchildren and I won't stand for it.' There were flecks of foam at the corners of the man's mouth.

Danny nodded absently, not bothering to discover who 'they' were supposed to be, because he wasn't really listening. Already in his mind he'd left the old man raving on the beach and had run, trailed by a crowd of vociferous seagulls, past the net-curtained bungalows and back to the hospital.

He turned away.

In the waiting room, things had changed. The receptionist, fluttering, kept calling him a hero and exclaimed over the flowers he'd bought from the florist near the hospital. A doctor appeared almost immediately and ushered him quickly away down a corridor.

'There was some smoke inhalation of course, some minor cuts

and bruising. We're keeping her overnight for observation – with any great exposure to carbon monoxide there's always the possibility of neurological impairment: cognitive dysfunction, short-term-memory effects, sensory motor problems.'

Danny nodded anxiously. 'But she'll be . . . ?'

'It's routine to keep her in overnight,' said the doctor.

Danny looked downwards and to the side, feeling awkward without the familiar hank of hair to hide behind. 'Do you know where Alice is?'

'Pardon?'

'Alice. She's Emily's cousin.' He paused and then hurried on, not wanting to think about the implications of what he was going to say. 'I think . . . if no one knows where she is then I think she might have been inside the house.'

'In the house, you say?' The doctor looked shaken. 'No one said anything about a cousin.' They stopped in front of a door. 'This is Emily's room, but if you'll excuse me I have to talk to the Inspector. God.' She blinked hurriedly. 'I'll let him know where to find you. I'm sure this will turn out to be a misunderstanding. Things like that happen more than you'd think.' Then she opened the door and waved Danny through before rushing away back up the corridor. He nodded slowly and walked into the room.

Emily was asleep on a bed by the window, eyelids faintly creased like tissue paper that had been unwrapped from around a present. Sitting beside her he was conscious that it was some time since he'd last washed. No one had offered him a shower and he smelled of smoke and sweat and still, faintly, of the muddy river. He wanted to stroke her hand or brush away the strand of hair that fell across her face, but, when she briefly opened her eyes, contented himself with a smile. Once, a nurse came into the room, made a hasty, scrawling note of something and then disappeared. Someone had found a vase for his flowers, and the tall orange daisies looked to be on fire in the sunlight. He covered his dirty face with his hands, sank a little lower in the chair and worried about what needed to be said to Emily, what she needed to learn about Alice. 'Walk through the door,' he muttered. 'Just appear now and walk through the door.'

He sat for a long time watching her sleep. In between worrying about Alice he felt strangely peaceful because it seemed that in saving Emily from the fire he'd at last fulfilled the promise of his miraculous beginnings underneath the ice. The scent from the daisies grew stronger in the room. She murmured something and shifted, and her unconscious hand made clutching movements on top of the sheet. He stared and just for a moment felt hot and cold, moving between two planes with the destabilizing sense of having gained something long-desired only to realize that he had merely ascended a level, like in a computer game, to a whole other frame which was filled with new doors and puzzles and rewards. Everything was about to begin all over again, and that knowledge was either terribly depressing or terribly hopeful. It was quite difficult, Danny concluded, to know what to think.

Walking on the beach in the midday sun she kept a lookout for drift-wood and for human remains. She found a plastic ice-cream tub, two old tin cans, a baby's nappy, a length of knotted orange rope, a coconut shell, one thonged sandal alone without its fellow. She kicked at the hard, dry, ghost-white skeletons of cuttlefish, the sort once collected by the painter Holman Hunt to make primer for his canvases. (The brightly coloured sheep on the grassy clifftop.) All that lengthily acquired knowledge when – who knew! – she should have been learning to build a raft out of pebbles, a ladder out of seaweed.

It was unconscionable, but no one had come; no one had found her. Where was the coastguard? The police? The authorities? Who-ever's job it was to make sure that people didn't disappear? Hadn't she always paid her taxes? Hadn't she, as a child, always coloured between the lines? In the morning she had stood with her back against the cliffs, staring out at the blank sea, and raged and wept and turned and beat her fists against the rock, but what was the point? *It's not faiiiiir.*

She walked to the west of the beach where the rocks were larger, darker, red-tinged and squarish in shape, like giant blocks of masonry stone, each one taller than her and with black crev-ices that seemed to run down for ever into the rocks like tears in the universe. Large insects, something like overgrown earwigs, scuttled away in front of her. All around, the cliffs rose up white, shading off at the top into brown, soaring like a cathedral. Beau-tiful and utterly remote in the bright sunlight. The muted, sterile palette of the landscape was only enlivened, here and there, by splashes of rock samphire – squat and bushy with umbels of yellow flowers, thick hairless stems and fleshy grey-green leaves. The rocks and the striated white cliffs felt very old and serious and quiet. She was like a child who had intruded into a forbidden adult world. Crouched down, out of the wind and buffered from the sound of the sea, the silence began to gather in intensity until she could hear two distinct tones – one low and one high – and she couldn't tell whether they came from the earth around her or from inside her body. The sound could have been caused by a dust particle trapped and echoing in the caverns of her inner ear or by an echo, only very faint, of all the noise in the rest of the world.

Because there was no one to talk to and therefore no way to discharge the accumulated sensations, she found that she was forced to live out fully each physical experience. In this littoral region she was more intensely, more completely, wet, dry, cold, warm, than she'd ever been before. When she closed her eyes and the sun hit her face she could feel the heat as a weight pressing down on her skin there, and there, and there. Because they had no companions, objects loomed large, took on greater import and significance. A knife in her hand was not just a knife but the knife. Her blue rucksack was essentially the very first blue rucksack in the world.

She would prize limpets off the reddish rocks and gather the samphire from the cliffs like a vision from *King Lear*. Where the stream running down the rock face fed into the ocean, bright green sea lettuce, thin and slightly sticky to the touch, grew on smooth pebbles. Underneath the waves there was dulce – purple-red with lobed, fan-shaped fronds, leathery but sweet – and flat brown strips of petal weed with the consistency of red liquorice. She would gaze out to sea and begin to comprehend how the water went on and on across the world for ever. She would be still at daybreak and let the sun sweep over her again.

Eventually, when she had been alone for long enough, there would be some feeling, some coming and going, that would finally stretch her out, she imagined, that would finally bring her to a place at the very edge of her self.

It was difficult to think about death in a landscape that afforded no sweeping, dramatic vistas, no sense of air, of sublimity. No hint in nature of the eternal or of the immense space that promised to open up after life. An elderly couple sat in their car, him behind the wheel, her in the passenger seat, a tin of boiled travel sweets between them. Unspeaking, they stared out at the sea, which today was brown and blue and slashed with hard, shining lines that formed diamonds on the surface. When the daily concerns of inland life seemed tiresome – families, neighbours, the opening of a flower – they could always come out here to the edge of the land to rest their eyes and minds, to practise looking at emptiness, at nothing. It was a consolation. Emily thought that they were brave to sit there. She couldn't imagine being that incredibly old and not wanting to jump off the edge of the cliff because, really, what good things were going to happen to them now? Emily no longer regarded herself as one of the young, quite, but there were limits.

She sneaked a glance at Danny sitting beside her on the bench. 'I'll look after you,' he'd said, holding her hand. She sighed. Then she blinked and felt more tears forming and wiped her eyes with the sleeve of the green jumper someone had given her at the hospital. It was several sizes too large and bobbled with age, but all the clothes she'd brought with her had been destroyed in the fire along with her copy of *Choose to be Happy*.

'My mother's booked her flight to come over with my aunt and uncle,' she said. 'It's so awful but I still haven't spoken to them.' Danny patted her hand consolingly as she broke into loud sobs. 'When will we *know* something?'

The police were saying that given the almost complete destruction of the wooden house, some sort of accelerant must have been involved, something that had really upped the intensity of the heat. They said that Ericsson must have been storing kerosene or something. The forensics team were in there, the police said, but it was taking time because the damage was so extensive. *It could take a while to find . . . to ascertain that there are no remains.* Ericsson herself was still in hospital. The doctors talked about exposure to cyanide – it would have been in the soft furnishings – and looked professionally anxious. The police had asked about Ericsson, about where she'd been, but all Emily had been able to say was that the artist must have returned to the bungalow during the night, after she, Emily, had fallen asleep.

Emily bent down to stroke Selkirk, who, unusually, submitted to her touch with only a flick of the ear. 'I keep going over what happened, but everything is so confused.'

It felt as though the smoke had got into her head and clouded up her brain. She felt stuffy. Stuffed up. The doctor had said that prolonged exposure to smoke could have neurological implications. She shuddered at a vision of herself as one of those short, dumpy figures blinking myopically and wandering around town with a paid minder. She would wear shapeless T-shirts and ill-fitting baseball caps in dirty white or faded navy and children would stare at her. *Mommy, Mommy, what's wrong with that lady's face?* The young could be so cruel.

'I remember I was dozing all afternoon.' She screwed up her eyes with the effort of memory. 'Alice went off for a walk and when she didn't come back I guessed she'd gone to town or something. I know it was early when I fell asleep.'

Emily vacillated. One moment she was certain that Alice hadn't ever returned – she would have woken up, she would have seen her – the next she was convinced that Alice had been inside the house with her. The police had made it clear that they intended to conclude their investigations at the accident site before launching any search. You could read something into that if you liked.

Danny leaned over to pat Selkirk and the dog snarled at him, flattening back its ears, and Danny let his white hand carry on down towards his plimsolls and fumble with his laces as though that had been his design all along. Emily wiped her eyes. Since waking up in hospital she'd felt also as though she'd shrunk in some way, as though she was quantifiably smaller in the world.

'Can I get you anything?' he said, eagerly. 'A drink? Something to eat?'

She shook her head. 'What about Alice's sister?' she'd said to the Detective Inspector who'd taken a statement from her. 'Don't you think it's strange that they're both missing?' He looked at her sadly. 'In my line of work, miss, strangeness is not irregular. It's seldom as meaningful as we think.' Then he yawned. It was warm and airless in the room they were talking in, and the windows were fastened shut.

The elderly couple, cheating death one more day, fastened their seat belts and reversed out of the parking space. Emily watched them leave. She realized that she now wanted most sincerely to go home because the world had grown dark and peculiar, and this new aspect would be easier to live with among the familiar blues and peaches and golds of California.

From the pocket of the jeans they'd given her at the hospital she extracted the pale yellow flyer that she'd found in the car. *Have you lost someone close to you?* the text began consolingly. She held it out to Danny.

'Look, this is from the car. It must have fallen out of Alice's bag.'

Danny took the flyer and scanned down the text. 'Guardian angels?'

'I never knew Alice was into this sort of thing. Angels. I never realized she was *spiritual*.' Emily shook her head. 'You think you know all about another person and then something like this happens and you realize that you don't know anything at all.' Emily had always thought her cousin rather cynical, but now it was becoming clear that Alice had been radically misjudged.

'Look!' said Danny, and he pointed to where a small, red-sailed boat was dancing up and down on the water. 'We should go on a boat trip,' he said. 'It will be a distraction.'

Oh, did she ever want to leave the island. She imagined herself flown away and happy back home among the wide and generous spaces. Watching the sailboat she caught a sudden childhood memory of Carol preparing to go out. She was staring at herself in the mirror, turning her auburn head this way and this way in the light, looking for something that Emily couldn't see. She stopped and walked over to where the girl was standing uncertainly in the doorway and crouched down so that Emily could smell the safe scents of coconut sun lotion and hairspray.

Close your eyes for the surprise, sweetie, Carol was saying. *Close your eyes now and hold out your hand for the surprise.*

Emily was giggling and Carol was talking. She was smiling and the smile was just for Emily and it was just the two of them together. And Emily, still giggling, closed her eyes and held out her hand.

Towards evening she crouched among the rocks on the beach. The skin felt tight across her face and the tops of her shoulders where it was burned red, turning brown. Salt crystals had formed on her eyelashes and thickened her hair. A rime of white decorated her cracked lips. White chalk was underneath her fingernails.

On the furthest, reddish rocks that stretched out into the sea were perched two black cormorants, hunched over like small, dark monks, but she was watching closer to the cliffs where a gull was bobbing over the pebbles. Its bright eye. She could almost feel the heat of the bird. As she watched, the gull began to seem more human, like a little man, bobbing up and down. Its eye was full of feeling. And she in turn was becoming more like a gull. Closer, closer. Her head twitched to one side and she felt her heartbeat speeding up. Suddenly the gull paused, opened its mouth to protest and took off into the air; out at sea a small yacht was crossing noisily in front of the beach.

She stopped transfixed where the gull had been walking. Her mind, which was becoming rock and chalk and feather, had groped backwards for an instant and thought that it had seen a figure she recognized on the deck of the small boat. She had seen blonde hair streaming out in the wind. But she knew it couldn't have been. She understood by then, with the part of her brain that still remembered such things, that her sister was only an idea, as lovely and intangible and heartbreaking as the clouds glimpsed through an aeroplane window.

The yacht disappeared around the headland and the sea became calmer. To escape the sun, which was too hot now, she huddled back into her shelter underneath the cliff. She was streaked with chalk from the rocks and she couldn't decide whether she needed to speak or be silent. The waves nibbled at the shoreline and there was nowhere else to go because the island was only part of a larger island, which was itself only another island, and Janey and Alice were little islands composed of even smaller islands, and the thought hurt like the idea of things impossibly small and impossibly large.

The day before she had looked down and noticed a small cut on her inner arm, in exactly the same place where Martin had worn a little patch of Elastoplast. *If I ever get back*, she thought, *I should give blood*. Wasn't there something miraculous about that? Something beautiful about the redness passing between strangers. There could be that at least, she thought.

Hello?

Do you hear me now?

Are you there?

She lay down and felt every stone pressing against her bare arms and legs and imagined being turned through a hundred and eighty degrees so that the stones pressed down instead of up and slowly, over thousands of years, compressed her skin and fat and muscle and bone into thick black oil.

When she looked up again, away to the west, the sea had turned red from the sun and it lapped at the chalky cliffs, and each time that it retreated she expected to see a fine pink tidemark staining the hard white bone of the island rock.

Acknowledgements

I would like to thank Andrew Kidd, my agent; Juliet Annan, my editor; and everybody at Aitken Alexander and Penguin, especially Jenny Lord and Caroline Pretty.

Also, thank you to Barbara and Simon Baker and Roy Robins.

He just wanted a decent book to read ...

Not too much to ask, is it? It was in 1935 when Allen Lane, Managing Director of Bodley Head Publishers, stood on a platform at Exeter railway station looking for something good to read on his journey back to London. His choice was limited to popular magazines and poor-quality paperbacks – the same choice faced every day by the vast majority of readers, few of whom could afford hardbacks. Lane's disappointment and subsequent anger at the range of books generally available led him to found a company – and change the world.

'We believed in the existence in this country of a vast reading public for intelligent books at a low price, and staked everything on it'
Sir Allen Lane, 1902–1970, founder of Penguin Books

The quality paperback had arrived – and not just in bookshops. Lane was adamant that his Penguins should appear in chain stores and tobacconists, and should cost no more than a packet of cigarettes.

Reading habits (and cigarette prices) have changed since 1935, but Penguin still believes in publishing the best books for everybody to enjoy. We still believe that good design costs no more than bad design, and we still believe that quality books published passionately and responsibly make the world a better place.

So wherever you see the little bird – whether it's on a piece of prize-winning literary fiction or a celebrity autobiography, political tour de force or historical masterpiece, a serial-killer thriller, reference book, world classic or a piece of pure escapism – you can bet that it represents the very best that the genre has to offer.

Whatever you like to read – trust Penguin.